*The Romantic Obsessions
and Humiliations of
Annie Sehlmeier*

# The Romantic Obsessions and Humiliations of Annie Sehlmeier

## LOUISE PLUMMER

DELACORTE PRESS/NEW YORK

Published by
Delacorte Press
1 Dag Hammarskjold Plaza
New York, New York 10017

A small portion of this book was first published under the
title "The Madonna Oma" in *Young Miss* magazine,
December 1986.

Manufactured in the United States of America

First printing

Library of Congress Cataloging-in-Publication Data

Plummer, Louise.
    The romantic obsessions and humiliations of Annie
Sehlmeier.

    Summary: After immigrating from Holland to live and
attend high school in Utah, Annie enjoys her sister's support
during the colorful experience until one special boy comes
between them.
    [1. Dutch Americans—Fiction.   2. Emigration and
immigration—Fiction.   3. Sisters—Fiction.   4. Utah—
Fiction] I. Title.
PZ7.P734Ro   1987      [Fic]       86-32795
ISBN 0-385-29574-X

J
Fic
P729r

# CONTENTS

PART 1: *America the Beautiful*     1

PART 2: *The Madonna Oma*     45

PART 3: *August Halloween*     71

PART 4: *Obsessions*     87

PART 5: *Humiliations*     135

PART 6: *Graduation*     173

# PART 1

## *America the Beautiful*

I don't like being an immigrant. I think of coarse-faced peasants in burlap pants carrying a couple of chickens in a basket and leading a goat down a gangplank when I hear "immigrant." Our family was never poor. We lived in a brick townhouse on Bernard de Waalstraat in Utrecht, Holland, and my sister Henny and I each had a bedroom of our own. My father was the head electrician at the Schouwburg, the opera house there.

What I like least about being an immigrant is that it means being conspicuous in public places. My father already thought that all the world was his stage and projected his voice consistently to the last row in the balcony. We hadn't even left Schiphol Airport in Amsterdam when he shrieked, "What have you got on your face?"

My mother, my oma, my sister Henny, and I stopped short in the middle of a KLM corridor and touched our own faces with one hand.

"What is that?" Father ran his finger across a dark brown

3

spot next to Henny's upper lip. I saw the lady at the information desk lean forward and stare at our family.

"It's a beauty mole." Henny's collected junk jewelry clanked lightly about her neck.

"A beauty mole?" Father looked at Mother, who pursed her lips. Oma reached forward to touch the beauty mole too, but Henny stepped back out of reach.

"Don't touch it. You might smear it," she said. She looked down her nose at my father. At sixteen, she was taller than he was. We were all taller than he was, except Oma.

"It looks cheap," Father said.

"I like the way it looks," Henny shot back.

"She wants to look like Madonna," I said. Henny sneered at me.

Father's face twitched with outrage. "She doesn't look anything like the Madonna," he spluttered. "She looks like a hooker."

"The rock star—Madonna—she's a rock star," I explained.

Father thought a moment. "Oh," he muttered feebly.

Henny guffawed. "You thought I was trying to imitate the mother of—"

"Never mind, Henny," Mother interrupted.

"No beauty moles," Father said, wiping vigorously at the spot.

"You're not being fair," Henny said through her teeth. "It's my face."

"No beauty moles," repeated my father. He folded his handkerchief and returned it to his pocket.

"Let's go," he said, grasping Mother's elbow and leading her down the hallway. "We should have stopped having children after Annie," he whispered loudly.

"Dirk," my mother cautioned him under her breath.

"I can't help it. She gives me heartburn." He pressed a fist into his diaphragm and burped right there in the airport. I could have died. "Why can't she be more like Annie?" His

4

voice rose to a high pitch which ended in a hiccup. He always compared Henny and me.

"Shouldn't we wait for Jacob?" Oma asked about her husband, my grandfather.

"He died fifteen years ago, Oma," I said.

"It must have slipped my mind," she said.

I took her hand and followed Mother and Father toward gate seven, toward a 747, toward Salt Lake City, Utah, United States of America.

Henny threw her flute case on the tiled floor.

*"Verdomme!"* she said.

If my parents had learned English, I might have felt differently, but my father was certain that all America was bilingual. Hadn't Govert, my father's older brother, lived in the United States now for twenty years and gotten along just beautifully? Hadn't Govert made a good living there as an electrical contractor and a Dutchman too?

"He must have learned English. I don't think many Americans speak Dutch," I told them both.

"Oh, come on now," Father returned. "Americans learn Dutch in school just like you girls learned English in school!"

"Father, I don't think Americans learn Dutch," Henny said. "Why should they? Holland is such a tiny country. In fact, there aren't that many Dutch-speaking people in the whole world." This statement brought on a rebuttal which included Dutch colonies past and present: South Africa, Indonesia, the Dutch Antilles, Peter Stuyvesant, and New Amsterdam. Probably all of New York City spoke Dutch like natives. America was raised up by Dutchmen and a handful of Englishmen. When he began on the influence of the House of Orange on the twentieth century, we stopped listening.

So, when we boarded the jet and the stewardesses spoke

Dutch, he looked at us and nodded and raised his eyebrows and made a fanfare with his face to let us know he was right.

But in New York, standing in front of a domestic airline counter, Father was surprised when the clerk, a young woman, didn't speak Dutch.

"We would like to check in for Flight 652 to Salt Lake City," said my father to the desk clerk. Her upper lip raised slightly, her face grew quizzical, and then she smiled, a dazzling smile—there must be good dentists in America.

"I beg your pardon," she said, leaning forward slightly as if she hadn't heard him.

"Ja, the flight to Salt Lake City," my father repeated in Dutch.

The young woman caught the "Salt Lake City" part and asked, "You want to go to Salt Lake City?"

"She can't understand you, Father," I whispered.

"She doesn't speak Dutch," echoed Henny, standing right beside me.

"Of course she can speak Dutch," my father exclaimed. "You can speak Dutch, can't you?" he asked the clerk, turning toward her.

"I'm sorry, I can't understand Norwegian," said the clerk, shrugging her shoulders.

"She doesn't understand you," hissed Henny. "She thinks you're speaking Norwegian! Let Annie do the talking now, pleeese."

Oma, who had been clutching onto her handbag with one arm and to my mother with the other, suddenly became aware of trouble. "Won't they let us into the country? Where will we go now?"

"She thinks I'm Norwegian?" my father asked me.

"Let Annie speak for you," repeated my sister.

"I've never been to Norway in my life," my father told the baffled clerk behind the desk.

"Father, for the last time, let Annie do the talking. That woman can't understand a word you're saying. *Now be quiet!*"

"Henny, you stop talking to your father like that right now," said Mother.

I stepped beside Father and swallowed.

"My father would like to check us into Flight 652 for Salt Lake City," I stammered to the attendant. I nudged Father, who handed her the tickets.

The young woman stapled them to a boarding pass. She wore a name card that said "Nancy." "Are you in the United States on vacation?" she asked me. She didn't sound anything like my English teacher, Juffrouw deWaart, who spoke with a clean, clipped British accent.

I told her we were going to live in Salt Lake City, Utah. We were going to be Americans. I was sorry I said it. My father picked it up immediately and said eagerly, "Yes, Americans," in his best English, which was poor, and pounded one fist on his chest to prove his allegiance to his new country. I was afraid he'd burp again. Henny's eyes rolled back in her head. Her fake jewels clanked with disgust.

The clerk smiled and looked us over from under the false eyelashes. Even without the goose in the basket and the garlic around the neck, I could see it too: we looked different. Foreign.

The minute the plane landed in the Salt Lake City airport, my nose began to bleed. I thought it was a cold and sniffed several times searching for a handkerchief in my bag. Passengers gathered in the aisles pulling down sweaters and jackets from the storage bins overhead. There was no handkerchief. In desperation I wiped my nose on the back of my hand. The smear of blood startled me. I plugged my nose with one hand and tried another vain search through my purse and skirt pockets. Father and the others were already moving down the aisle.

"Stay close together," he ordered. Mother held Oma's hand. A drop of blood trickled down my wrist.

"Wait," I said. A short woman wearing dangling jade earrings jostled me as she passed. Fat drops of blood turned to rivulets on my hand. "Wait," I cried again. "I need a handkerchief." I was practically hemorrhaging.

"Use your hand," said Henny without turning to look at me.

"Mother!" I yelled. She was at least half a dozen persons away up the aisle. Everyone turned to stare. Mother sent a handkerchief down to me via several fellow passengers. A man with a red mustache, listening to our foreign chatter, mused to his wife that we were probably Hungarian. The blood cascaded from my nose.

Father and Mother waited in the jetway leading to the terminal. The other passengers jostled past us. Mother's handkerchief was already soaked, so Father handed me his.

"What could have brought this on?" he murmured.

"There's Ome Govert and Tante Geert," cried Henny. She pointed to the end of the tunnel where Govert and Geert, their faces leaning forward, smiled at the sight of us.

Father waved at them vigorously and led us into the terminal. He shook his brother's hand and then embraced him. Govert had the same high cheekbones and ears as Father, but was much older and balder.

"You've gained weight," they blurted together, each tapping the other's stomach. They laughed at themselves.

"Not me." They each said it and guffawed over this second coincidence. But I thought they had rehearsed the whole thing when it happened a third time: "Just like twins," they each said. This made them so hysterical they crumbled against each other for support. Frankly, they looked like a couple of drunks. Everyone in the place was looking at us again.

Meanwhile, Mother and Tante Geert had exchanged hugs and kisses. Tante Geert was teary-eyed and fat. Not that those two necessarily go together, but I just noticed then that she was fat. When they had visited in Holland seven years before, she was still a thin, almost slight woman. I couldn't believe the change.

"Mama, you remember Geert, Govert's wife, don't you?" Mother pushed Oma tentatively forward. Geert was about to kiss her, but Oma shrugged back and said, "No."

Geert, not rebuffed, tried a reminder: "Oma deWitt, don't you remember, you had a party for Govert and me when we were married at your house in Breukelen."

Oma clasped the brooch at her throat as if it were about to be stolen. "I did not!" she said.

Geert drew back and squeezed Mother's hand. The attention turned to my nose. "Annie, are you all right?" she asked, kissing my cheek, the part farthest from my nose.

I nodded and smiled uselessly from behind two blood-soaked hankies. I felt like a soft-drink dispenser.

"What an awful thing to have happen on your arrival," said Ome Govert.

"Some people will do anything for a little attention," said Henny.

"Is this little Henny?" shrieked Tante Geert. She was really pretty fat. I don't know why, but it embarrassed me. She grasped Henny's shoulders. "I can't believe it, Govert." She nudged him with her elbow. "Can you believe this is little Henny? I can't believe it. You're so grown up. You're both so grown up. How did you do it?"

"We just kept breathing," said Henny. She kissed Geert's cheek.

Tante Geert leaned close to mother. "I guess they've both started their periods," she whispered too loudly.

Henny rolled her eyes upward and groaned. I turned toward the window. The air rippled hot above the silver body of the airplane.

"We'll stop in the bathroom on the way out and I'll make you a cold compress for your nose," said my aunt. "It will clot the blood," she said.

I shrank back. I didn't want this fat, sweating woman to hover over me this way. I didn't want to be related to her. She grasped my arm cheerfully and pulled me toward the corridor. "We'll meet you by the luggage in a few minutes," she called to the others. "Hold your head back," she instructed. "Yes, that's a good girl."

We drove east into Salt Lake City in Govert's Buick station wagon. Oma, seated between Mother and Father, immediately fell asleep, her mouth evidently open because she snored like a warthog, occasionally causing her false teeth to click. I was never going to be old.

Henny described the landscape: "Motels everywhere. There's another one," she said.

"That block is Temple Square." Ome Govert pointed. "That's the Mormon temple."

Ome Govert and Tante Geert had come to Salt Lake City after joining the Mormon Church through missionaries in Holland. He and my father had fought over this decision.

"I thought it was the Dutch Reformed Church," Father said. He gave a little "Heh, heh, heh." We all gave a little "Heh, heh, heh," in relief.

We stopped for a street light. A blond boy wearing a T-shirt with IS IT FRIDAY? written on the front crossed in front of the car. I leaned forward to get a better look, but Tante Geert pushed my head back onto the seat.

"Isn't he darling," admired Henny from the backseat.

The adults snickered. "A real peach," said Ome Govert.

"We have better-looking boys in our neighborhood," said Tante Geert.

"Better-looking than him? Wow. America the Beautiful," Henny sighed.

"Tante Geert meant me, Henny," Ome Govert called back. He and Father had identical "Heh, heh, hehs."

It seemed to me that Henny had a dramatic recovery from her black despair at leaving Toby Visser behind in Utrecht. Not two days before she howled right through supper, claiming her life would be unbearable without him and now here she was leering at a perfect stranger on the sidewalk. Henny could be so disgustingly juvenile.

When the light turned, Ome Govert turned left, apologizing, "This isn't the way home. I just want to show you this one block. That's the church office building with the fountain in front of it." He pointed at a white high-rise. "I want you to see the gardens." He slowed the Buick and stopped briefly in a No Parking zone. "See the tulips."

I strained my neck to see the gardens. There were thousands of different-colored tulips.

"Dutch tulips," he said. "The church orders them all from Holland."

"Looks like the Keukenhof gardens," Mother breathed. Her voice threatened to crack.

"Makes you a little homesick, doesn't it?" Tante Geert asked in a soft voice.

Ome Govert took us right through downtown, past the elegant, white-bricked Hotel Utah, a department store with the odd name of ZCMI, down Main Street, a wide thoroughfare of shops, banks, restaurants, and movie houses. *Back to the Future* with Michael J. Fox was playing at the Utah Theater. I loved American movies and movie stars. I liked Jane Fonda and Amy Irving, Harrison Ford and Robert Redford. Kaatje, my best friend, and I used to go with Edo, her older brother, and watch old movies at the university where he was a student. We saw Clark Gable and Claudette Colbert, and Fred Astaire and Ginger Rogers. Edo knew everything about the movies. He knew who directed what, who designed the sets and the costumes. He could even dance certain steps and for some films like *Gone With the Wind,* he was able to mimic whole scenes, playing Scarlett O'Hara in a falsetto voice and then, turning aside, change to Rhett Butler with a twitch of his upper lip. I loved Edo. My favorite movie star was Meryl Streep, whom I considered intellectual. I also thought I looked like her. I had this calendar called *Stars* with Meryl Streep on the cover wearing no makeup. I looked just like that picture except my nose was a little shorter and my eyebrows were thicker, kind of like Brooke Shields's. I had this special little eyebrow brush to brush them upward. Kaatje used to say she'd kill for my eyebrows.

From Main Street we turned up 8th South, which became a considerable hill and eventually turned into Sunnyside Avenue.

"We live off this street," Ome Govert told us. He said Emigration Canyon was just a few minutes away by car. I leaned forward to see Emigration Canyon and weighed in my mind if mountains compensated for the loss of the North Sea and the reassuring green flatness of Holland. I wasn't sure.

We turned into Avon Street. I sat straight up now, my nose having stopped bleeding. Feelings of nausea hovered in my throat. Tante Geert kept one arm around my shoulder. We passed a white house for sale on a corner, with a dark green front door and a brass knocker. The backyard had a patio shaded by a birch tree, except for one sunny corner where pots of petunias squatted. The lawn was neatly trimmed. I wanted to live in that house, on this block, with its well-kept yards and tiny brick houses and trees. This neighborhood had trees. Trees were important.

"There's a house for sale!" Henny saw it too.

Mother and Father strained for a glimpse of the house.

"Can we go look at it?" Henny persisted. "We can look," said Father. "But that doesn't mean we can afford it. We're not rich, you know."

We continued another couple of blocks and stopped in front of a modest but pleasant two-story stucco house. Evergreen bushes flanked either side of the front steps.

"This is home," said Ome Govert, pulling the keys from the ignition.

Mother and Geert escorted Oma into the house. Henny and I helped Ome Govert and Father unload the luggage from the rear of the car.

"Hi, Mr. Sehlmeier!" A tanned boy wearing a headset rode by on a ten-speed. At the sound of a young male voice, Henny bumped her head on the roof of the car. She rubbed the wound and watched him pedal down the street.

"Who was that?"

"Flash Garrett. He delivers our morning paper. Nice boy except when he misses the porch."

I thought "Flash" the dumbest name I'd ever heard for a human being.

"Every morning?"

"Yes."

"He must have to get up very early to deliver papers," Henny continued.

"I guess so."

"How early, do you think?"

"Our paper's always here by six."

Henny watched the street thoughtfully although the boy had long since turned the corner. "America the Beautiful is no joke," she breathed.

That was when I threw up in the street, splattering Ome Govert's immaculate white Buick station wagon.

Henny awoke me by holding a cold orange against my neck. "You've slept sixteen hours. That's long enough," she said when I swatted against her.

She sat on top of me.

"What time is it, anyway?" I sat up.

"Five o'clock."

"In the morning?"

"Yes." She grabbed my pillow to prevent my lying down again. "Let's go look at the house that's for sale. It's only a couple of blocks from here."

"Now? At five o'clock in the morning?"

"The traffic's light. Hardly anyone on the sidewalk." She lifted a lace curtain and peered down the street. "Can't see a soul," she muttered.

I wanted to see the house again and stand on the edge of the lawn, a tentative proprietor.

A dull thud sounded from below. Something had hit the side of the house.

Henny's head perked up at the sound. "We have to go right now," she said. She pushed me out the door and past the bathroom. "Shh." She gestured with her index finger in front of her lips.

"Let me at least tie my shoes," I said.

The morning newspaper lay on the front steps, folded and held together with a thick rubber band. Henny picked it up and held it to her breast as if it were a gift from a lover. The neighborhood smelled freshly scrubbed.

"This way," she said. She sprinted across the lawn, still carrying the newspaper. I ran to keep up with her.

"Henny," I called. She was really running fast now. "The house is the other way."

"I know," she said. She was almost at the corner when she stopped. It was then that I noticed it. I would have seen it sooner, but I hadn't been sufficiently awake. Henny was dressed as if a movie contract depended on it. Instead of

14

wearing jeans, she wore a dress and sandals, and her face was painted with the full Elizabeth Arden assortment of cosmetics: lipstick, blush, eyeshadow, and eyeliner. One tiny Madonna mole had grown overnight, it seemed, next to her bottom lip. She primped her perfectly placed hair and searched the next block.

"You tricked me," I said fiercely. "You said we were going to the house. You're looking for that paper boy, Lightning, or whatever his name is." I was grinding my teeth.

"His name is Flash," Henny said. "Oh, Annie, I just want to meet him, but I don't want to go alone. Please," she pleaded. "I'll go look at the house with you in a few minutes."

She had taken such trouble with her face and hair. Her head was almost a work of art. "What are you going to do?" I asked.

Henny accepted my question as a positive answer and tapped me lightly on the arm with the newspaper. "I'm going to pretend he dropped this paper and give it back to him," she said.

"What's he going to think when he sees the way you're dressed? Isn't he going to wonder why you're out at five o'clock in the morning looking like Krystle Carrington?" I asked.

"We're on our way home from a slumber party."

"That explains the way I look, but it doesn't explain you." My own hair was knotted and limp. I was sure I still had dried blood around my nose, and my mouth exhaled straight beagle's breath.

"I'll think of something," said Henny. "Come on, I think he went this way." She pulled my arm. We turned the corner. Flash was nowhere in sight.

"He's turned the corner again," Henny sighed. We jogged together in lock step, past several houses.

Suddenly a large burly man in a navy bathrobe sprang out

15

at us from behind a tall hedge. He waved a baseball bat above his head.

"Now I've got you," he shouted. "Stay right where you are. You're not getting away with this any longer." He continued waving the bat, his feet spread solidly across the sidewalk.

Henny and I screamed and clutched each other. I could hardly breathe.

"You've stolen my newspaper for the last time. Give it to me!" He reached with one hairy paw for Ome Govert's newspaper.

I wasn't sure Henny understood him, he talked so fast, but she clutched the newspaper tighter and backed away.

"Give it to me, you female juvenile delinquent." He moved forward.

"We're from Holland," I offered meekly. I tried to stand behind Henny so he'd hit her first.

"I don't care if you're from Idaho. Nobody's going to steal my paper for two weeks in a row and get away with it. Give it here," he demanded.

"No!" Henny shouted. She was catching the gist of the conversation after all. "No!" She yelled it again. That's the whole problem with Henny; she's tenacious.

"I think we should," I whispered. I have no moral fiber or righteous indignation in dangerous situations.

"No."

"Call the police, Maggie," the man roared, waving the bat above his head.

"Daddy, they're not the ones." A girl's voice yelled from an upstairs window beyond the hedge row. I saw her plainly: dark, chin-length hair and large, owly glasses.

"Call them, Maggie," the man shouted back.

I felt a thick warm trickle cross the line of my upper lip.

"Your nose is bleeding," the man said in an entirely new voice. He lowered the bat for the first time.

16

"You did it!" Henny yelled at him. Life in America was beginning to feel like life in a blender.

"I didn't do anything," the man said. "I didn't touch her."

"You scared her. Call the police," she called to the girl in the window.

"Henny, don't." I wiped the blood with my fingers. The window banged shut.

"I didn't do anything," the man said. My nose streamed blood.

"You try to kill her. You have a gun too?" Henny continued.

"Will you please be quiet." The man glared at Henny. "You're worse than a roomful of mosquitoes." To me he said, "Lean your head back. Maybe that will help." This seemed to be the universal solution for nose bleeds.

"Daddy, they're not the thieves." The girl from the window appeared breathlessly from behind the hedge. "I saw them come from way up the block with . . ."

"It's okay, Maggie. This is my daughter, Maggie Connors," he said.

She nodded and smiled shyly, I thought. She wore a long, red, wrinkled T-shirt with UNIVERSITY OF UTAH in large white letters on the front. She looked worse than I did, I decided. She handed me a wad of Kleenex. I accepted them gratefully.

"I'm Annie Sehlmeier." I stammered. "This is Henny, my sister. Govert Sehlmeier is our uncle."

They didn't recognize the name at first. "Oh yes," Mr. Connors said. "Damned good electrician. Sorry about the bat," he said. "Someone's been stealing my paper and it's driving me crazy."

Henny snorted and then her eyes widened as Flash Garrett coasted around the corner. Two empty newspaper bags sagged against the side of his ten-speed. He stopped along-

17

side Mr. Connors and pulled off his headset. Maggie hid behind her father.

"I saved your newspaper for last," said Flash. "I was going to ring your doorbell to make sure you got it today. Great legs, Maggie," he said pushing off on his bike.

"Thanks," Mr. Connors called after him. "G'bye, girls. Come around again and we'll play baseball." He swung the bat onto his shoulder and waddled like a bear around the side of the hedge.

"He didn't even notice me," Henny sighed.

"Who?" Maggie asked.

"The paper boy," I said.

"You wanted Flash to notice you?" She inspected Henny. "Wow. You really did want him to notice." She giggled. "You look too good," she said. "You should have stapled a pepperoni pizza to your bosom." She exploded the word "bosom" and we all laughed. The three of us stood in a perfect square of sunshine. My nose stopped bleeding; a good omen, I thought.

Kaatje Tefsen
Domstraat 18
Utrecht, The Netherlands

Dear Kaatje,

I'm here! Can you believe it? I've been in America twenty-four hours. (Tell Edo, no, I haven't seen Mel Gibson yet, but I'll let him know when I do.)

I'm sitting in Ome Govert's backyard at a picnic table nursing the third nose bleed since I got here—it's the altitude, everyone says. Actually, I'm hiding from Tante Geert, who hovers over me like some mammoth nurse whenever I bleed. She is fat as a dinosaur. Many layers of prehistoric flesh hang from her upper arms. I wish you

18

could see her. You could do a great drawing of her. I would draw her myself if I weren't such a hopeless artist.

I haven't seen much of Utah yet. I saw the Great Salt Lake from the jet, and we drove past the Mormon temple and the gardens and through the rest of downtown just briefly, but that's all. I can see the mountains from here, "purple mountains' majesty." You would love them. The sky is clear blue. It almost never rains during the summer, Ome Govert told me. I won't know how to act without drizzle.

Everyone says I speak terrific English. I met a girl this morning—Maggie Connors—she couldn't believe I hadn't been here before. (Tell Juffrouw deWaart that she's a fantastic English teacher.) Although I made the most horrible mistake today with Ome Govert and Tante Geert. The three of us were out in the backyard and Ome Govert began complaining about this huge tree. "A trashy tree," he called it, because it dropped all kinds of seeds and muck on the lawn. Anyway, I volunteered in English to *"rape* the lawn" for him. Tante Geert just burst out laughing. Ome Govert kind of scratched his head, grinned and said, "That might be harder than you think." I still didn't get it. Finally, he said I could *rake* the lawn but I ought not to try *raping* it. I felt like a total fool.

Henny and I found the most wonderful house for sale just a few blocks from here. I can't explain it. It just feels right. You know what I mean? We begged Father and Mother to come down and look at it, but so far they haven't.

Please, *please* write me. We will be staying with Ome Govert and Tante Geert until we get a house of our own (let it be the white house!). I will let you know the new

19

address. Tell Edo to send a postcard. (Does he ask about me?)

Kiss, kiss, kiss,
Annie

I wanted to say more in the letter about Edo: Tell Edo I love him and have loved him since I can remember. Tell him I know he's too old now but that in a few years it won't matter anymore. I will be adult soon, very soon. Tell him to wait. Wait for me Edo, with your beautiful Indonesian face and dark curly hair. Wait.

At supper Father announced that we were going to rent a house and not buy one. "We have to watch our money." He repeated it twice.

We sat in the kitchen around a wooden drop-leaf table with the leaves extended. All of us sat, that is, except Tante Geert, who was cooking up enough dinner for a whole boatload of immigrants and sweating over it. Her sweat really bothered me. I accepted the plate farthest from her armpit.

"What do you mean we can't afford it? We have money," Henny said, loading her mouth with mashed potatoes. Her face was washed clean. No beauty moles at dinner.

"We have enough money to rent a modest house," explained Father, emphasizing both "rent" and "modest." "We need furniture, for heaven's sake."

"And a piano," I interrupted. "We need a piano."

"That house down the street *is* modest," Henny persisted. Go, Henny, go!

"Besides, it's close to relatives and," she looked at me with just the beginning of a smile, "and it's close to friends."

"It's a perfect house," I said.

Father wiped his chin with a paper napkin, and then his nose. "I repeat," he said firmly, "we cannot buy a house at this time. Govert has made an appointment for us to see a house that we can rent this evening."

There was a pause while Henny and I collected ourselves. Ome Govert remained silent behind his newspaper. The big chicken.

"Where is it?" Henny asked first.

"It's down the hill on 8th South," Tante Geert said. She was eating her own dinner, standing, her mammoth hip leaning into the stove.

We had come up 8th South the day before. I remembered it. A wide street, almost like a highway. I didn't want to live on a highway.

Bad things come in threes. That's how I knew we would live on that highway. It all added up to three: 1) being an immigrant with what seemed more and more to be the most modest of means; 2) a house on a highway; and 3) living on a street without a name—a numbered street—8th South. The only thing worse could be an odd number. I especially hated odd numbers.

A half an hour later, when we stopped in front of the house-within-our-means, I was faced with the final humiliation: the house was directly across the street from a junior high school with a chain-link fence surrounding it, and the number of the house was odd. I felt my life changing in a way I couldn't control when I saw that junior high school. As if bad things didn't just come in threes anymore, but in dozens or swarms or herds or gallons or millennia.

The house itself was a pleasant brick, with similar houses on either side of it. It had a wraparound front porch with pink climbing roses blooming on the front porch railing. The front door had a large glass inset, curtained with a faded, yellowed drape. Mother noticed the drape, and I knew by her face that she would remove it when this was her house.

Ome Govert led us onto the porch, where we stood in a

21

cluster. We looked like a convention, all of us crowded on that porch. I began to wish I hadn't come.

"The real estate agent will meet us here in a moment," mumbled Ome Govert. "She just lives a few blocks from here."

Mother seated Oma in one of the green, metal rockers. The setting sun was still bright, a desert sun. A faint breeze blew the fragrance of roses into our faces. I tried not to think of those roses and the porch, both of which I liked. I wanted to be grouchy just a while longer. I looked across at the chain-link fence. It didn't actually surround the school; it went around the grassy playing field adjacent to the school. One might almost think of it as a meadow.

"Hi, are you people going to rent the Swensons' house?" a nasal voice sang across the shrubbed hedge dividing our house from the house next door. Already I thought of the house in a proprietary way.

I peered across Ome Govert's shoulder and saw a very skinny girl about my age, possibly younger, with the curliest head of bright orange hair, I mean *orange* orange, that I had ever seen. One hand was on her hip, the other shaded her eyes. She chewed gum, a whole pack at least, in a slow rotating motion, the tip of her tongue darting visibily at the edge of her mouth.

Henny answered, "We're looking."

"Oh, we could use some girls in this neighborhood. Just boys here now."

"Really?" Henny's interest perked.

"Yeah, but they're all weird."

"Oh."

Makes no difference if they are, I thought. Henny prefers weird.

"Are you sixteen?"

"Yes."

"Me too. I'll be a junior this year."

"I will be in the eleventh class," Henny said.

The girl thought for a moment. "That's junior year!" she exclaimed. "Sounds better as eleventh class."

They squinted at each other in the sunlight.

"I'm Farrah," the girl said. "Farrah Spivack."

"Farrah. Like the actress," Henny noted.

"Yeah! She used to be a model, you know." The girl stepped closer to the hedge.

"We love American movies, especially Farrah Fawcett ones," Henny said.

Speak for yourself, I thought. I couldn't even remember seeing a Farrah Fawcett movie.

"You look a little like her," Henny said.

A bald lie. This girl looked nothing like Farrah Fawcett except that she had arms and legs. Henny liked her. I could tell. She was courting this girl for a friendship. Henny was good at making new friends. How could she overlook that head, blazing like the inside of a furnace?

An American car—a Chevette—I read on its side, stopped in front of the house. A middle-aged woman in a gray suit, carrying a man's briefcase got out and slammed the door. "Mr. Sehlmeier?" She looked between Father and Ome Govert.

"I am—that is—we both are. My brother here doesn't speak English yet," Ome Govert said.

"I'm Mrs. Gensmer." She shook hands with Ome Govert and nodded at Father.

"Is this woman showing us the house?" Father asked loudly.

"Hi, Myrtle." Farrah waved from her front lawn.

"Hello, Farrah," said Mrs. Gensmer briskly, not even turning her head. "What language do you people speak, anyway?"

"They speak Dutch. They're from Holland," said Ome Govert.

"Oh, Dutch tulips are my favorite kind," she said, as if we were flowers. She pulled a set of keys from her purse and searched until she found one that unlocked the front door. Mother and Oma stood now.

"Just follow me in," she said to my father as if he could understand her.

"Just follow me in," my father said to the rest of us in Dutch. Henny and I couldn't help but snicker. All of us followed him into the house.

Henny held back and called to Farrah: "Come and go through with us," she said. "You can tell me about school and things."

Mrs. Gensmer talked non-stop whether anyone listened or not. It seemed to make no difference to her that the prospective renters couldn't understand a word she said. "That was the vestibule that you just passed through, and this is the dining room." We stood in a large, unfurnished room with high ceilings. A large, oddly shaped brass chandelier hung in the center of the room. To the left of this room was the living room with three large windows that overlooked the street. "Lots of light as you can see," continued Mrs. Gensmer. "This is a very light house. Not at all depressing, don't you think?" She nudged my mother in the arm. Mother, startled, nodded back and smiled at her. Oma nodded at her too.

"She says it's a sunny room," I whispered to Mother.

"I met someone from your high school this morning," I heard Henny saying. She and Farrah were still standing in the vestibule. "At least, I guess he goes there. Flash Garrett."

"Oh, did you meet Flash? He's a good friend of mine. Flash is cool." Even in the living room, I could hear her chomp on her gum.

"Flash is cool," imitated Henny and then laughed.

"Are these plaster walls or dry wall?" Ome Govert asked on his way to the kitchen.

"Are utilities included? What about water?" whispered Tante Geert to Govert. "Ask her."

"The stove and refrigerator are included, of course," Mrs. Gensmer was saying.

I looked out the living-room window across to the junior high school. Look on the bright side, I thought to myself. Living across the street from a junior high school is better than living under a railroad bridge. It's even better than living above a barber shop. Maybe. The street wasn't quite as wide as a highway and our side of the street, at least, was lined with elm trees, although the other side was bare. It was so far from perfect. So far from what I had hoped for myself in America. So near and yet so far from the house on Avon Street. I didn't bother holding back a sigh. This house and neighborhood were a disappointment.

We followed Mrs. Gensmer through two bedrooms downstairs and then upstairs to a single bedroom at the front of the house. It was a large room with sloping eaves and a pleasant floral wallpaper.

Mother's mouth was frozen into a polite smile, and her head nodded automatically now at Mrs. Gensmer's stream of information, none of which she understood. "Henny and you could have this room," Mother whispered to me out of the side of her mouth.

"Are there other kids our age in the neighborhood?" Henny was asking Farrah. They were just now walking up the stairs.

"Jack Wakefield lives around the corner, a short block away. He's your sister's age."

"Does he have a girlfriend?"

"No." Chomp, chomp, chomp. I really didn't like this Farrah with the orange hair.

"Where's Oma?" Mother's voice rose above the general hubbub. Father and Ome Govert were exploring an attic storage area at the back of the house. Tante Geert had been translating for Mother and Mrs. Gensmer—something about carpeting, and Oma had left.

"Dirk, is Oma with you?" Mother called to Father.

She wasn't.

"What's the matter?" Farrah asked.

"My grandmother's missing," Henny explained.

"Maybe she wanted to see the kitchen again," Farrah said.

"I doubt it," Henny sighed. "Come on, we've got to find her."

She and Farrah were first down the stairs. The older women followed. Father rushed out into the hallway at the top of the stairs. "Where is she? Have you found her?"

"No, they're looking downstairs."

Father hurried so fast he almost tripped getting to the stairs.

Ome Govert paused at the top of the stairs. "Does Oma disappear like this often?" he asked me.

"Well, she didn't used to. She kind of goes in streaks. Sometimes she's perfectly okay." I thought for a moment. "But not very often, anymore."

Henny and Farrah came in the back door.

"She's not in the backyard," Henny said in Dutch. "Or in the garage either."

"I'll look out in front," I said. When I stepped out onto the porch, I saw her almost immediately. She was standing on the sidewalk directly in front of the house next to Farrah's. Two houses down. It was a much larger house than the rest of the houses on the block, as if it had been the first in the neighborhood and was later joined by the other smaller houses.

I called through the screen door to my mother who was still in the kitchen. "She's out here," I said. "She's all right."

Oma stood very still, staring up at the second floor of the house, her handbag clutched to her chest.

"Oma," I said, touching her arm. "Everyone was worried

26

about you. We didn't know where you'd gone." Mother and Geert were already coming down the sidewalk.

"Annie, I saw Jacob," she said, meaning my grandfather—her husband.

"What?" I asked.

"I saw him. He lives in this house." She was speaking to Mother and Geert, who were standing with us now. "All this time he has lived in this house."

"Oma, that's not possible." He's dead, I wanted to say. I looked up to where she was looking and gasped. Mother and Geert saw him too. There was a man sitting at a desk by an open window who had the same shape head and white hair as Opa had. He turned his face to us and poked his head out.

"Is something wrong?" he yelled from the window. He really didn't look that much like Opa. He had finer features. Certainly the hair, the way it was combed, was very similar.

"No, sorry," I called back.

Oma raised both of her arms up to him. "Jacob, come back to me," she cried passionately, if that's possible in an old woman. I wouldn't have thought so before she said it like that. "Come back to me," she said again in Dutch.

"What is she saying? What does she want?" asked the man. He was now leaning way out the window.

"She thinks you're her husband. Sorry. She's ill. She doesn't know."

Mother and Geert tugged at Oma, but she didn't want to leave. Mrs. Gensmer, Henny, and Farrah now joined us.

Why was it always like this? We hadn't been in this neighborhood ten minutes, and we were already a spectacle.

"What's the matter with your grandmother?" Farrah asked Henny.

"She's just crazy," Henny said matter-of-factly.

"Don't say that." I glared at her. "She's ill," I said.

"She's ill and it makes her act crazy." Henny corrected herself and sneered at me.

"The poor thing," Tante Geert commented. "She thinks that man is her husband. Poor thing."

"Mr. Eberley?" Farrah laughed. "That's a riot!" She snorted.

I really didn't like her one bit.

Oma wouldn't leave Ben Eberley's sidewalk. She began wailing in a distressed and awful manner, Mother and Geert trying to persuade her to leave all the while.

"Ben, maybe if you'd leave the window, she'd let us take her back," Mrs. Gensmer shouted up to him.

Mr. Eberley stared at Oma for another brief moment and then gently shut the window and drew the curtains.

"Now I've found him, and he doesn't want to see me," Oma cried. "Oh, Jacob." She bawled into a handkerchief, but at least she let mother and Tante Geert lead her back to the car. Mother got her seated in the backseat. Geert volunteered to sit with her so that Mother could finish looking at the house. "It will be all right," she said, when Mother hesitated. She pulled the door shut. Mother walked back to the house.

Farrah, Henny, and I sat on the front porch steps. We could hear Mother explaining the whole incident to Father, who interrupted her with questions like, "What did the man do?" and, "Was he angry?" I leaned forward, cupping my head in my hands, my elbows on my knees, and watched Oma cry in the Buick. "I think the sky is bluer here," I said, breaking the silence on the porch.

Farrah looked up. "I've never been anywhere else except Thatcher, Idaho, so I wouldn't know. The sky's very blue in Thatcher, too. Here comes Jack Wakefield," she said, looking down the hill. "Remember, I told you about him. He lives around the corner." The boy called Jack rode a red Honda scooter with a grocery bag in the white wire basket in front. The hill was steep. He slowed down when he neared the corner.

Farrah called to him before he turned. "Come here a minute," she yelled. He glanced at his watch, drove onto the sidewalk, up the front walk, and released the kickstand.

"They're going to be at East High next fall," Farrah said, nodding at us. "They're from Holland and they might, just might," she crossed her fingers and held them up, "move into this house. This is Annie and this is Henny. Like Henny Penny." She laughed. "This is Jack Wakefield, who probably won't speak to you again after today." Farrah wrinkled her nose coyly at him. "He never talks to me—the meanie."

"Glad to meet you." Jack nodded at us. He was tall and already quite tan, although it was only early June. His hair was sandy and cut short at the sides. His face was—it was a lovely face. A rather serious face. "Do you speak English?" he asked us.

"Yes," Henny and I said at the same time.

"Do you speak Dutch?" Henny asked him.

"Only a little German—is that close enough?"

Henny grinned. *"Nicht so gut wie Holländisch, aber wir können Deutsch sprechen."*

*"Was sollen wir auf deutsch besprechen?"* Jack asked without so much as a wince.

*"Sag' uns, warum wir in dieser Nachbarschaft wohnen sollen,"* I said.

"What are they saying?" Farrah wanted to know. "Is that Dutch?"

"It's German. Annie just asked him why we should live in this neighborhood," Henny explained.

*"So dass ich Deutsch sprechen kann. Ich muss gehen. Meine Mutter wartet auf diese Lebensmittel,"* Jack said.

"What?" Farrah's mouth hung open.

"He says we should live here so that he can speak German with somebody."

"Nice meeting you." Jack switched to English. "I'll probably see you again." He shoved the scooter off its stand and pushed it backward to the sidewalk. "What's your last name?" he asked me.

"Sehlmeier," I said.

"Isn't that a German name?"

"Yes. We're not pure," I said.

"Glad to hear it." He laughed aloud. I wasn't sure what was so funny. "See you later." He sped around the corner.

Suddenly this seemed like a splendid neighborhood. It seemed like the very best neighborhood I could think of. On a scale of 1 to 10, this seemed like an 11. Jack Wakefield lived around the corner somewhere. I got up.

"He's cute," Henny said.

"He's okay," Farrah said.

"I think I'll go in and see if they've decided anything about this place," I said.

"Tell them to take it," said Farrah.

I found Mother in the backyard inspecting raspberry bushes. I hugged her from the back. "Are we going to live here?" I asked.

"Do you want to?" she asked, turning around.

"Yes, it'll be all right," I said.

"What about that other house that you and Henny had your minds set on?"

"This is okay," I said. "Henny likes that girl, Farrah. They're talking on the porch like they've known each other all their lives."

"You'll find a friend too," she assured me. "Someone as nice as Kaatje."

"I like Maggie," I said. "She doesn't live all that far away."

And I liked Jack Wakefield.

We stayed with Ome Govert and Tante Geert for another week. Father went to work with Ome Govert for part of each day, and then he and Mother shopped for furniture.

Maggie called on Sunday afternoon and asked if I would

like to come to her house for some dessert. Actually, she asked for both me and Henny, but Henny had been invited to go for a drive in the canyons with Farrah.

"Will your father be there?" I asked. He was dangerous as far as I was concerned.

Maggie laughed. "He's harmless. Really," she said. "Don't worry, I'll protect you. Come over now."

Maggie's house was a substantial colonial. She answered the door herself and pulled me into a large center hall with a winding staircase that led to the second floor.

"What a beautiful house," I breathed. It was stunning. Maggie took my arm and pulled me into the living room. "I want you to meet my parents," she said. "Daddy promised to be on his best behavior," she whispered. "Okay," she announced in a loud voice to her parents seated on a white sofa. "We're going to start all over again with Annie. Daddy, Mom, I want you to meet Annie Sehlmeier, who is from Holland and will live on 8th South as of tomorrow."

"Hello, Annie." Mrs. Connors stood up and wiped her mouth with a napkin and shook my hand. Both of them had been eating a lemony-looking dessert. Mr. Connors set his plate on the coffee table in front of him and stood too. In his best formal manner, he bowed, and said, "How do you do, Miss Sehlmeier. I'm very happy to meet you."

Maggie laughed and I couldn't help smiling. "I am happy to meet you too," I returned. He looked much different with his face shaved smooth, his hair combed, wearing dress slacks with a shirt and tie. Mrs. Connors was quite beautiful. Maggie had her father's darker coloring.

"Sit down, both of you," Mr. Connors ordered. Maggie and I sat on a loveseat together.

"What part of Holland are you from?" asked Mrs. Connors.

"Utrecht."

"We were there!" she exclaimed. "It's a lovely place.

31

Don't you remember, Bill? We climbed all the way into that tower of the old church."

"The Dom," I said.

"I remember. Practically had a coronary," Mr. Connors muttered.

"We stood up there and looked out at all of those red-tiled roofs. It was lovely." She clapped her hands together. Mr. Connors looked amused at his wife's enthusiasm.

"She liked the catacombs too," he said. "Do you still get nosebleeds?" he asked.

"Three times since I've been in America."

"America makes you bleed, huh?" He smiled at me. Maybe he wasn't a gorilla after all.

"Now don't play doctor," Maggie yelled at him.

"What a wonderful piano," I exclaimed, hoping to change the subject. I didn't want to talk about my nose or my blood. Besides, I sincerely admired the black piano that dominated the other side of the living room.

"Do you play?" Maggie asked excitedly.

"Yes, do you?"

"Yes. How long have you played?"

"Ten years."

A slow smile grew on her face. "Will you play?" she asked. "I mean, do you have anything memorized?"

It was a test. It felt like a test, not an unfriendly test, but a test nevertheless. She wanted to know how well I played. I understood that. I was just as curious about her. There were pianists and there were pianists.

"Yes," I said. "If you'll play for me."

"I will," she said.

"Good." Mr. Connors smacked his hands together. "A mini-recital in our own living room."

"Annie, you don't have to play if you don't want to." Mrs. Connors hurried in. She turned to her husband. "We haven't

32

even fed her yet, and now we're making her play the piano. What kind of hosts are we?"

"We'll eat afterward," Maggie insisted, her face excited. She wants me to play well, I thought.

I sat down on the piano bench and looked at the keys for a long while. I would play a Brahms ballade for them. It's what I played when I won the student competition in Utrecht. Not having played in several days, my fingers felt stiff. I began. The piano felt alien, like some unfamiliar machine I was supposed to make some sense of. I felt panic. But then, as the music, mine and Brahms, filled the room, filled the whole house, the keys became familiar and warm under my fingers. The bass notes rolled clear, separate, together, separate, *prrrum pum pum pum, prrrrum, pum pum pum.* The fragrance of lavender blew in through the open French doors. I liked playing in this house—for these people. The key changed, the music grew softer, romantic, floating up, not a wasted note, floating and lingering and pining, always pining the way I did. Pining for perfection.

When I finished, the three of them sat dazed until Mr. Connors broke the silence with, "Hell's bells, that deserves a bravo if anything ever did." And he stood up and cheered, and Maggie and her mother clapped too, Maggie grinning from ear to ear, repeating, "Oh, it was just wonderful—it was super!"

I had passed the test. I bowed a low exaggerated bow and moved away from the piano. "Your turn." I gestured to Maggie.

"Thank you, Maestro." She sat down, her back perfectly straight, and waited for us to sit down.

She played a Mozart sonata, clear and happy like Maggie herself. She made it look simple, and I knew it wasn't. Her playing was artful and intelligent. I wanted her for my friend. When she finished I clapped heartily. "Encore," I yelled. She really played splendidly.

"Let's play duets!" Maggie had already moved to one end of the bench.

"First pie," demanded Mrs. Connors. She cut a piece out of a round tin, placed it on a saucer, and handed it to me with a napkin.

"I have heard of pie," I said, "but I've never eaten it. Apple pie. I have read about American apple pie."

"This is lemon pie. They all have the same crust, which is supposed to be light and flaky." She wrinkled her nose as if she had doubts about this crust.

I liked the lemon pie with its light meringue cover that melted on my tongue. I liked everything about the afternoon, the house, the music, Maggie's parents, and Maggie herself, so earnest in those owly glasses and so friendly. I was glad I hadn't had to share any of it with Henny for once.

When Mr. and Mrs. Connors left for a walk, Maggie and I played duets and sang popular songs, Maggie taking the soprano and I, whenever I could identify it, the alto.

"You have to sing in senior choir," she said to me.

When we tired of singing, we sprawled out across two beds in Maggie's bedroom. One wall was completely covered with books. She had many books I had read in Dutch translation.

"Do you like to read?" she asked me.

"All the time, especially novels," I said.

She turned on her stomach, her chin propped in her hands. "You're too good to be true," she said. "You sort of fell out of the sky, playing the piano, singing, reading, all the things I like, and you look like . . ."

I hoped she would say Meryl Streep.

"Like a Dutch princess."

"I like you too," I said honestly. "I like your parents, your beautiful house, your American lemon pie. I think you should adopt me."

She giggled. "I'll speak to Daddy about it tonight," she said. "Have you read this?" She pulled a tattered paperback book from one of the lower shelves: *The Thorn Birds* by Colleen McCullough.

I shook my head.

"Oh, you must read it. It's so wonderful. It's also a television movie with Richard Chamberlain—the heroine's name is Meggie and it's all about forbidden love." Her eyes widened. Forbidden love was better than ordinary love. "I've got it on video and have seen it a million times. The book's better, though." She forced it into my hands.

She turned onto her back. "List all the boys you have loved since first grade," she commanded. We both watched an insect crawl across the ceiling.

"First class: Janntje Vander Broek. Second class: Henk Osterberger. Third class: Peter Brinksma." I continued listing them to the ninth class, Maggie amused at the foreign-sounding names.

"What about the last three years?" she asked.

"Peter Brinksma again," I lied. It was Edo. Kaatje's brother Edo. He was the one I really loved, but he was eight years older—too old for now. It was so silly. I was six thousand miles away from him and I still didn't dare say his name aloud. "He never knew I was alive," I said. "Silly, isn't it?"

"Infatuations. That's what my mom calls them. Most of mine are infatuations too." She began listing them. I listened, enjoying the names, until she hit fifth grade: Jack Wakefield.

"Jack Wakefield? He lives by our house," I said. "I met him." I felt myself blushing. Maggie either didn't notice or was too polite to comment.

"Jack's nice. Smart too," Maggie said.

I wanted to say, "Tell me everything about him. Does he have a girlfriend?" But I said nothing.

"He doesn't have a girlfriend," she said slowly. "Isn't that what you wanted to know?"

I swatted her with *The Thorn Birds* across the space between the two beds.

She held her glasses in place with one finger. "I can read your mind," she said. "It's a gift."

"You can't read anything. Go on with your list."

"Mac takes up the rest of my list. Walter McBride. Everyone calls him Mac." She reached in back of her and took a framed picture from the stand next to her bed. "This is Mac," she said, handing me the picture. "Even my mother is beginning to believe that this is not infatuation." She wiped some dust affectionately from the frame as I held it. "He's not really what you call handsome, but he's smart as Einstein. Almost." She giggled nervously. "He just left with his family for England. He's going to Oxford next fall while his dad is on sabbatical. His dad is an English professor at the U."

"The U?" I asked.

"The University of Utah."

"He looks nice," I said, looking down at the photograph. "He looks like you." I laughed. He had the same dark hair, a wide-open grin, and dark-rimmed glasses.

"Everyone says that. I think it's the glasses." She pushed hers back on her nose. "I'm getting contacts at Christmastime and then maybe we won't look like the Doublemint Twins anymore." She kissed the photograph gently, then wiped it with her sleeve, and set it back on the nightstand. "I love Mac," she said simply. "We're going to be married someday. He and Jack Wakefield are best friends, by the way." She blinked both eyes meaningfully at me. "Thought you might be interested."

I swatted her again. I wished I could claim Edo that simply. Edo and I will be married someday.

Maggie walked me home. "I want to meet your parents and your grandmother," she said.

"They don't speak any English, you know."

"I'm good at sign language," she said.

We cut through backyards and alleys. I told her about Kaatje and mentioned Edo briefly. It felt good to say their names aloud in America. I didn't know where we were until she pressed a wooden gate, barely visible between the lilac trees, and we were standing in Ome Govert's backyard. The kitchen was lit up. Mother, Father, Ome Govert, and Tante Geert sat at the table.

"You can hardly tell they're Dutch." Maggie pointed at the wooden shoes nailed along the side of the back door. They had new geraniums planted in them.

"They probably never wore them in Holland," I said. We entered the kitchen, which smelled of chocolate.

I introduced Maggie to everyone.

*"Aangenaam kennis te maken."* Father and Mother shook her hand.

"It's a pleasure to meet you too," Maggie said, without waiting for a translation. It seemed to be the truth. Ome Govert pointed at two empty chairs. Tante Geert pushed a plate of chocolate-chip cookies in front of us. We each took a couple. The plate had a substantial chip in it. Maggie didn't seem to notice it. "These are delicious," she said.

*"Goed?"* asked my father.

"Gch, gch, gch, yes!" Maggie said. The rest of us laughed.

Oma walked in through the swinging door. Her hair fell down her back, below her waist. She wore a nightgown and a little pink knitted bed jacket that Henny had knitted her for Christmas last year. She looked like an aged Ophelia.

"It's so silly," Oma said in Dutch, "but I can't find the bathroom."

I got up quickly. "I'll help you," I said in Dutch.

"You stay here, Annie," Mother said. "I'll take her up."

"She has such beautiful hair," whispered Maggie.

"Oma, Maggie thinks your hair is beautiful," I said to her in Dutch.

*"Dank je wel."* Oma smiled sweetly at Maggie and waved good-bye. Mother took her away.

"It's fun to hear you speak Dutch," Maggie said. "Your parents are very nice, and your Oma too."

"She's senile, you know."

"I know. You told me. Do you miss her? The person she used to be?" she asked me. I thought it a most astute question.

"I do," I said. "It's like two separate people. Two different omas."

"I can imagine," she said.

Ome Govert and Father stood up. "We have to go pick up a truck for your father at the shop," Ome Govert said.

"How do you say good-bye in Dutch?" Maggie asked me. *"Dag."*

*"Dag,"* she said to my father. It sounded like dak. He laughed.

*"Dag, dag."* He waved as they went out the door.

I sighed with relief. It hadn't been as perfect as Maggie's house, but it had been fine.

"I have to go too," Maggie said. "Thanks for the cookies, Mrs. Sehlmeier," she said to Tante Geert. "I'll see you again, Annie." She touched my arm lightly. *"Dag."* she smiled.

*"Dag."* I waved her out the door.


The next day we moved. There wasn't that much to move because most of the furniture had been delivered, including a new black studio piano, which sat against the wall of the dining room. It was by far the most expensive piece of furniture they had bought and I was grateful and said so several hundred times during the day.

"It's just a wonderful piano—I thought we would get an old beat-up thing. I thought we didn't have any money," I said. I was washing down woodwork in the kitchen with Mother and Henny.

"If I had played the piano, I'll bet we wouldn't have gotten

38

a new one," Henny pouted, dripping water alongside her bucket.

"You have a good flute," Mother said.

"Flutes don't cost as much as pianos."

"Oh, for heaven's sake, Henny." Mother finished scouring the sink.

Henny had been irritable since the piano had arrived. I was happy. Nothing she said could bother me today. Henny and I cleaned the bathroom while Mother scrubbed and waxed the kitchen floor.

"What did you and Farrah do yesterday?" I asked her, trying to get her mind off the piano.

"Rode around through the canyons. She let me drive the car a little," she said. "We can get a license, you know. It's a lot easier than in Holland. You can even take driver's lessons at the high school."

"I bet Father won't let us."

"He can't stop me," Henny said. "Let him try. All the kids here drive. I saw Jack Wakefield drive by this morning. He waved at me."

*So he knows that we've moved in,* I thought.

Ome Govert and Father came to the back door carrying the kitchen table, a chrome and plastic-looking thing with six ugly matching chairs.

"What do you think?" Mother asked when it was all set up in the middle of the room. She had laid a vinyl cloth over the table.

"It looks fine," I said. "I would have preferred a wooden table."

"It looks very easy to keep clean," Henny said.

Mother pressed her lips into one tight angry line.

"I'll get some flowers for the table," I said.

"All right, but nothing messy," Mother called as I went out the door.

At the front of the house, late tulips bloomed along the hedge close to the Spivacks'. I picked several.

"Do you speak English?" A woman stood on the Spivacks' porch. She held a baby in one arm and a wrapped loaf of bread in the other.

"Yes," I said. Her hair was in curlers covered with a bandanna. She wore a baggy pair of corduroys with bulging pockets.

"I'm Irma Spivack, Farrah's mother." She stepped down off the porch and walked over to me, handing me the loaf of bread. The baby squirmed in her arms.

"That's for your family. Tell your folks welcome to the neighborhood. I'll speak with them when they learn English." She stepped back onto the porch and disappeared inside her house.

"Farrah, have you practiced the piano yet?" She screamed inside the house. "Farrah?"

Several neighbors welcomed us that first day. Miss Rifkin from the corner house brought an apple cake with raisins in it, and asked if we had a dog. She seemed relieved when we told her no. Mrs. Keddington, who lived across the back alley, brought divinity, white, little peaked clouds of soft candy spooned onto a platter. I had never eaten it before, but I ate three pieces immediately. "Let's learn how to make this stuff," I told Mother. Mr. Eberley left a plant on the front porch with a note of welcome attached to it. Jack Wakefield's father came by to say he was the bishop of the Mormon church around the corner and if we wanted to attend church there, we were certainly welcome. I translated back and forth between him and my father, blushing the entire time. Father shook his hand vigorously and told Bishop Wakefield that his brother was a Mormon but he thought he'd remain a member of the Dutch Reformed Church. Bishop Wakefield said he understood. Then he helped my father carry a swamp cooler from the garage and install it in the dining-room window, showing him how to fill the cooler from the back with the hose. I didn't stay with them the whole time. They seemed to get along somehow with a kind of pidgin Dutch. Jack's father was a tall man, handsome for his age. Jack looked like him.

Henny and I organized our bedroom upstairs. We divided the room in half, running a line of masking tape down the center of the floor and up a bookcase. We divided the chest of drawers and the closet. "If I see any of your stuff on my side of the room, I'll throw it out the window," Henny warned me.

"Same here," I said. I was much neater than Henny. If she wanted to make a stupid rule like that, let her go ahead. As far as I was concerned, she was shooting off her own foot.

The room was wallpapered with small flowers in pink and green with a cream-colored background. Mother had bought two cream-colored bedspreads and green throw rugs for the floor. The window had a wide sill, not really a window seat, but wide enough to sit on in any case. I sat looking down on the street.

"Your feet are on my side of the room, Miss Piano Princess," Henny pointed out.

I withdrew my feet. Henny was such an irritating child.

At the end of the day, Tante Geert and Ome Govert brought Oma down in the Buick along with a pot of pea soup which we inhaled. My father insisted that we inspect our home in America so we all followed him, single file, while he pointed out all our possessions, beginning with a second-hand lawn mower in the garage and his white Toyota truck with SEHLMEIER ELECTRICAL CONTRACTORS painted on the doors. We walked through the kitchen, already cleaned up from dinner. He opened all the cupboards to show us the dishes. He opened the drawers to show us flatware and linens. We walked through the downstairs bedrooms, into the dining room with the piano and the dining-room table and chairs. The living room had a new divan with a matching chair and a recliner for my father in front of the television. He sat in the recliner and showed us how it changed from a chair into a lounge. We had all seen it before. Two teak end tables held familiar trinkets from Holland and the plant from Mr. Eberley. Mother's old lace curtains hung in the living-room and dining-room windows.

Upstairs, Father and Mother were not amused with the masking tape running across our room, although Ome Govert and Tante Geert found it funny; but then they don't have any kids.

"I'm just keeping the peace," Henny explained when Mother and Father glared at her.

When we were back in the kitchen, Tante Geert prodded Ome Govert. "This is a good time—now," she said.

"Oh." He jumped up from the kitchen table. "We have a little surprise. I'll be right back." He went out the back door.

"I hope it's a convertible," Henny said.

Mother distributed lemonade to everyone and leaned against the counter.

Ome Govert carried in a large box.

"It's a microwave oven!" Henny leaned forward in her chair.

"Got it on sale at Kmart," muttered Ome Govert. "Just a little housewarming present. I'll show you how it works," Ome Govert said, and began boiling water in a cup, which took all of a minute.

We all sat down around the new microwave, which sat temporarily on the kitchen table. This was our first night in our house in America. Across the street, the Little League battled it out on the playing field of the junior high school. Next door, Farrah Spivack played a limited version of Grieg's "Piano Concerto." She played the first page again and again. Someone ought to do a mercy killing on that girl, I thought.

Inside the house my family, including my aunt and uncle, watched water boil in our new American microwave oven.

Kaatje Tefsen
Domstraat 18
Utrecht, The Netherlands

Dear Kaatje,

No, we're not rich now that we live in America. Did Edo coerce you into asking that? It sounds like him. People do live well here, though. I mean, take our new (75-year-old) house for example; it is a modest house by American standards, yet all the rooms are much larger than our house in Utrecht, as is the yard. Americans seem to take space and the size of things for granted. I mean refrigerators here are enormous, with huge freezers in the top and then besides that, everyone has a mammoth freezer in the garage. We do too; it came with the house. Mother is simply baffled by all of these oversized appliances. Tante Geert said she would get used to them. And she would get used to the huge supermarkets too and buy groceries to last a month instead of a couple of days.

The best example of American excess, though, is the car. Everyone here owns at least two cars. I mean everyone. Mr. Wakefield, who lives around the corner, is a wallpaper hanger (and a Mormon bishop on his off hours, but he doesn't get paid for that), and his wife teaches nursery school part-time. They have two cars, a pickup truck, and a scooter which their gorgeous son Jack rides. My new friend Maggie Connors has a car of her very own and so do each of her parents. Her father's a doctor. The Spivacks next door have two cars and a truck. There's good bus service inside Salt Lake, but Maggie said she wouldn't be caught dead riding the bus.

Farrah Spivack (oink, oink) had the same attitude toward public transportation: "Riding the bus is the pits," she told me in those exact eloquent words. They let kids drive at age sixteen. I can't believe it. I'm kind of afraid, but I'd like to learn.

It is incredibly hot and dry. The hotter it gets, the more people water the grass. Green lawns are a source of extraordinary pride here. I like to sit on the porch in the evenings and listen to the water blow through the sprinklers on all the front lawns down the block. Across the street, on the playing field of the junior high school, the sprinklers all go on at the same time every afternoon. It looks like a mist in a fanciful ballet.

I'm bored. Wish you were here to share things like my new black piano, and my suntan, and my white moccasins bought at ZCMI. I feel shy about calling Maggie to do things. I don't know her that well, and I'm always afraid I'll be taking her away from her other friends. Maybe I'll call her after I'm finished with this letter and ask her advice on a piano teacher. I really need to get to work. I'm losing it fast!

What did you mean, "Edo is really flying high these days"? Drugs or women or both? Tell him to send me a postcard. Have to go—I promised Mother I'd walk to the grocery store for her. *Dag, dag.*

> Kiss, kiss, kiss.
> Annie

P.S. I had another nosebleed yesterday—filled a whole dishtowel with my precious blood. Mother says if it continues, I'll have to see a doctor. Groan.

# PART 2

## The Madonna Oma

IN some other world, not the one I lived in, beautiful people gathered in the evening, sat on their satin-covered bottoms at a table decked out in Lenox china and ate a civilized meal of exotic dishes like breast of unicorn. Their eyes feasted on unpronounceable flowers—anemones and forsythia—bunched artfully in silver urns. I knew it existed. I saw it in a glossy magazine and I wanted a perfect life like that. Photographs don't lie. Do they?

We ate in the kitchen on a table spread with a vinyl cloth that Henny and I wiped down with a damp sponge after the dishes were cleared. Our eyes feasted on linoleum. Yet our kitchen had a glittering cleanness about it that I appreciated, and Mother hid the dirty pots and pans in the oven while we ate dinner. That *was* civilized. It was the dinner conversation, or rather the lack of it—the spats—that depressed me, and they were Oma's fault. She was the cause of our mealtime fights. Like the dinner when Jack Wakefield called me on the telephone for the very first time.

Oma was refusing to eat, her lips held shut in a stubborn,

tight line and Mother simply wouldn't let it be. She was afraid Oma might starve herself. Fat chance. Oma ate Oreos on the sly.

"Please have some soup now," my mother pleaded, soup spoon poised in the air in front of Oma's clamped lips.

Oma, her arms folded across her chest, turned her head away from Mother. Her hair fell loose from the knot in back of her head. She looked unkempt, like pictures of old people in rest homes I had seen. Sometimes, I thought she smelled different too—not a good smell either.

"Open up wide," Mother said. You'd have thought she was talking to a one-year-old.

Oma shut her eyes, wrinkled her nose, and did not open her mouth wide.

"Eat your dinner now, Riet," Father said, buttering a roll. "She'll eat when she wants to."

"She never eats," my mother said.

"She eats all day," said Henny. "She's in the refrigerator whenever she thinks no one's looking. She ate all the Twinkies last week."

"She's not going to get better if she doesn't eat properly," Mother insisted, implying that Twinkies kept one senile and the minute Oma changed her diet she would be herself again. I couldn't believe it.

"Eating is not going to make her better," Henny said. "Nothing is."

Mother offered Oma a buttered roll.

"I hate it," said Oma in Dutch, through her teeth.

"Then *I'll* eat it," said Henny, snatching the roll from Mother's hand. "I love them."

As soon as Henny bit into the roll, Oma wanted it back. If she was not interested in eating she was interested in possession, and it was *her* roll.

"Give it back," she shouted. "It's mine."

That was when the telephone rang.

"Give it to me." Oma cried.

I got up and answered the phone which sat on a small table in the hall adjacent to the kitchen.

"You don't want it, so I'm going to eat it," said Henny.

"Hello," I said into the receiver.

"Tell her to give it back!" Oma yelled. She began wailing.

"Hi, this is Jack."

"Jack." Unbelievable. Old Spice aftershave seemed to waft through the telephone receiver. Jack Wakefield was calling me.

"Henny, stop teasing your grandmother," Mother said.

"Can we eat in peace, for once?" Father asked Henny.

"How are you?" asked Jack.

Not fine. Not fine at all. And marvelous. Never felt better. All of the above.

"Fine," I said. The kitchen was exploding with noise.

"What's going on?" he continued. He could hear everything, I was sure of it.

"Oh nothing," my voice was serenely casual. "My grandmother sometimes gets upset at dinner." I put one finger in my free ear.

"Your grandmother?" he asked. I could hardly hear his voice.

"People who don't eat, don't get anything," Henny taunted Oma. She picked up the entire basket of rolls and held them above her head.

Oma, frantic, howled like an animal.

"Henny!" My father's balled-up fist smashed the table surface. Dishes clattered.

"Are you eating dinner?" Jack asked.

"No. I mean, yes. Can I call you back in a few minutes?" I couldn't believe I was making this request, but Oma was bawling so loudly, I couldn't concentrate on his voice. I didn't want him to hear her. I didn't want him to hear my whole crazy family.

49

"Okay, I'll talk to you in a few minutes then. Bye." I was sure he had heard everything. Good-bye, my love. Jack Wakefield had called me and I couldn't talk to him.

"Why should the rest of us have to listen to her whining all through dinner?" Henny shouted at Father.

"You make it worse when you tease her." Father's hands were still fists. It occurred to me that he wanted to punch Henny and even though I was mad at her too, the thought made me sad. We were so far from those Lenox china advertisements.

"I can't stand it," Henny screeched. "Every night Mother begs her to eat. Just let her alone!" She had turned to Mother.

Oma had parts of three rolls stuffed into her mouth, chewing on the dry bread and watching Henny to make sure she wouldn't get them back. Fat crumbs fell from her mouth onto the table.

"See, *now* she's eating. Are you satisfied?" Henny pushed her chair back and stood up. "You don't have to beg her." She sneered at Mother. "You just have to steal it from her."

"Henny, sit down!" Father's face was white.

"I will not sit down. I hate this family. Hate it, hate it." She knocked her glass of milk over, swerved around to the back door and was gone. The walls shook with the door's bang.

For a second we all watched the milk spread across the vinyl cloth and drip into Oma's lap. Oma began crying all over again. The rest of the bread fell from her mouth.

"I'd like to kill her," Father said. I believed it.

"Let her be," Mother said. Her head nested in her hand. "It's not her fault." She shaded her eyes with her fingers.

"Then tell me whose fault is it?" exclaimed my father. No one answered. I had never seen him so mad. This was dangerous. I felt it.

It is Oma's fault, I thought. I wiped the table and Oma with a dishtowel and told her to hush. She continued weeping noisily. *I wish you would die now.* A part of me—the good part—was shocked and sorry I had thought such a thing; but another part agreed that it was Oma, as she was now, who was the center of these all too frequent fights. I tried hard to remember the Oma of before, her hair thick, humming morning hums that nurtured a small girl. Oma, picking asters out of her garden on Poortstraat and arranging them perfectly in a blue delft vase. Oma, my link to the civilized world of the glossy magazines. There was a light about her then, like Madonna paintings; or was that my imagination? This woman, this present Oma, weeping and choking on bread, her nose running—she wasn't the same person even. There was no resemblance between the two. This person was the one I wanted to die. Not really, of course. Not really. I hope I didn't mean it. Mother's head was bent over the table. *I didn't mean it Mother. Erase. Erase.*

Erase it with Jack Wakefield. I pictured Jack's family dining in formal clothing, drinking wine from Waterford crystal. I returned to my place and ate my soup in silence.

After dinner, I sat with Oma out on the front porch while Father and Mother attended English lessons at the junior high across the street. Henny had not returned. I was sure she was hiding out at Farrah's until she cooled off. Henny almost lived over there lately. I had tried to call Jack once, but the line was busy. Now I was stuck with Oma. We couldn't leave her alone. She either grew frightened like a child, calling loudly for my mother or she wandered off down the block, forgetting the way home. Often she sat on Mr. Eberley's porch repeating my grandfather's name. Once Mrs. Spivack, our neighbor, had called to say that Oma had walked into her house and was napping on her bed.

We sat in the green, painted metal chairs behind the porch railing and the climbing roses. The neighborhood smelled clean, green. *The Thorn Birds,* the book Maggie had lent me, rested in my lap. I hoped to read it while we sat. Already I wanted the handsome priest, Ralph de Bricassart and the young Meggie Cleary to become one flesh, as it said in the Bible. At least I thought that's what it said in the Bible. Colleen McCullough was not going to gratify me too quickly on this score. Oma was humming softly. I picked up the book. She stopped humming.

"Do you remember me—what I was like—before the car accident?" I was startled by this completely lucid question from her. She was so crazy most of the time. I lay the book down again.

"I used to read a lot too," she mused.

"I remember," I said. It was only a vague memory.

"You are a lot like me," she continued. I wanted to disagree and perhaps she saw this in my expression because she added, "The way I used to be. You are like I used to be." I thought again of the asters in the delft vase, but I couldn't think of anything to say. She wanted a response from me, but I couldn't make one.

"You even look like me." She stroked my cheek briefly and then looked out to the street. A blue Ford truck burning a lot of oil sputtered its way up the steep hill.

"I was young once," she repeated. "Like you."

"Annie, hi!" Jack Wakefield's red scooter jerked to a stop at the curb in front of our house. He wore white shorts and a T-shirt and held a tennis racket. He parked the scooter and walked to the porch.

Oma's face hardened immediately at the sound of his voice.

"Jack!" My voice didn't sound like my own. "I tried to call you but the line was busy." I pulled my feet down from the porch railing and tucked my skirt modestly under my legs.

"I know. My brother Milton was on the phone. I decided to stop by on the way to the courts." He glanced at Oma. "I'm Jack Wakefield." He extended his hand for Oma to shake. Oma sat tight-lipped and stared straight ahead.

"She's senile," I whispered. "And she doesn't understand English." I didn't want him talking to her. I just never knew how she would react. It was bad enough having her sit there like a stone. My face felt about two hundred degrees, and I was sure my neck was developing those ugly red splotches. Soon he would know that I was a person susceptible to rashes. Unclean.

"Oh, I'm sorry," Jack whispered back. He smiled at Oma and nodded to her. He was irritatingly polite.

"You're going to play tennis," I said, trying to veer his attention away from Oma.

"Yes, I'm meeting Tom Woolley." That was the first time I heard Tom Woolley's name. Jack's tall frame leaned against the porch. "I was wondering if you'd like to . . ."

*"Geef hem niets te eten ook al bedeld hÿ er voor!"* interrupted my grandmother. I felt my neck definitely redden. No question about it.

"What did she say?" Jack asked.

"She said not to give you anything to eat, even if you beg for it," I said. I would have made something else up if I could have thought of anything.

"Tell her I just stopped by to say hello," he said.

"Let's just ignore her," I said quickly. "She'll stop if we ignore her."

"Annie, she's your grandmother." Jack had a wretched respect for the elderly. "Tell her," he insisted. He made a gesture with his hand that indicated I should get on with it.

I told Oma that Jack had come by to visit us both and that he didn't want anything to eat. Jack seemed pleased to hear me speak Dutch.

Oma jumped to her feet with surprising vitality and waved her fist fiercely at Jack, who drew back involuntarily. "Liar," she yelled at him in Dutch. "You've come to steal the potatoes and leave us here to starve. Get out. Get out of here." She leaped forward to the stairs. Jack backed down the front

53

walk. Oma grasped the garden hose, turned the spigot and aimed the spray directly at him, catching him full in the face. Jack dropped his racket and spluttered, "But I'm not even hungry." He started the scooter and sped awkwardly away.

"She thought you were stealing potatoes," I called out after him, but he was gone.

"You stupid woman!" I turned on Oma. "You stupid, stupid woman." I yanked the hose from her hands and wrapped it imperfectly around the spout next to the porch. "How could you do such a thing?" I yelled. Her disheveled head was bowed, her shoulders sagged. She reminded me of an abused dog. I wanted to hit her.

"Go in the house," I said, picking up Jack's tennis racket off the lawn. I wiped it with my skirt.

Oma stood inside the screen door looking out at me. "He'll come back to get it," she said plainly and disappeared into the house.

I hoped it was true.

Across the street, on the playing field next to the school, a man in white pants and shirt guided a model airplane by remote control. It buzzed in the air like a tin insect. I wanted to fly too—spell Jack's name with my white breath across the sky. I wanted to be transformed into some magnificent glittering creature in a silver, sequined gown by Bob Mackie, who designs dresses for movie stars, and gauzy wings designed by God, and hover over the neighborhood while ordinary mortals like Farrah Spivack stared at me in awe, calling my name, pleading for my autograph from the sidewalk below.

I walked into the house. Oma sat asleep in the recliner, her jaw hanging slack, arms folded across her stomach. The skin on her hands was loose and translucent, the blue veins bulging in a way that made me shrink back. My own hands were smooth as porcelain, the veins only pale blue lines mapping the surface. Then I noticed it. The veins in my hands were the same configuration as Oma's. Exactly. I held my hand, fingers spread, close to hers. Exactly the same. "You are a lot like me." Oma's words boomed in my head. "The way I used to be." I fought the idea that her hands were ever as smooth as mine. I fought the possibility that someday I might be old and forgetful and that someone young and smooth and pretty as Meryl Streep would yell at me and call me "stupid."

Quietly, so as not to awaken her, I covered her with a knitted afghan. I covered the hands that were like mine, and remembered the other Oma, the Madonna Oma, holding me on her lap. I leaned forward and kissed her face. "I still love you, Oma," I said.

Lingering behind lace curtains I watched the street hoping that Jack would return, but he didn't come. The only thing left to do was eat. I pulled a new bag of Oreo cookies out of the drawer and made a pitcher of iced tea and set them down on the card table on the back screened-in porch. The neighborhood was quiet except for the occasional buzzing of an insect and the rhythmic swishing of the Spivacks' sprinkler next door. I opened my book and then opened an Oreo and licked out the center. Australian sheep shearer Luke O'Neill had just proposed marriage to the fiery Meggie Cleary when I heard Henny's shrill screech coming from the Spivacks' back porch, followed by Farrah's loud laughter and piggish snorts.

"I'm going to die," I heard Henny exclaim. More screeching. She was obviously fully recovered from her dinnertime rage.

"I told you he was totally awesome," Farrah exclaimed. "Don't you think he's better-looking than Mel Gibson?"

"Geez, yes." Henny made a strangled noise. "I'm just going to lie down here and die!"

*Let me help you,* I thought. The pear tree blocked my view of the Spivacks' porch, but I pictured Henny and Farrah jumping and flailing themselves around the four walls and occasionally bouncing off each other. Henny let out another piercing scream followed by, "I'm in love. Hopelessly and deeply in love."

I made a silent, cynical list: Toby Visser, Peter deVries, Jantje Bissell, Wilhelm van Valkenburg, Gerard Dicou, and Theo van Kaiserswaard. She had been hopelessly and deeply in love with each one of them too.

"Farrah, the baby is asleep. Please be quiet or go outside." This was Mrs. Spivack's impatient nasal voice coming from inside the house.

The two girls, trying to muffle their laughter with their hands, stumbled out to the backyard and fell onto the grass, where I could see them. I stuffed the bag of Oreos ungraciously under a chair pillow and tried to read again.

"I wish school started tomorrow. I wish I could go out with him. I wish I had a picture of him," Henny gushed.

I wish you would eat rocks. I closed *The Thorn Birds,* laid my head on my forearm, and watched a ladybug crawl precariously around the rim of the iced-tea pitcher.

"Kid, I have pictures—yearbook pictures and one or two others. Wait here." I heard Farrah go into the house and return shortly.

"Here they are. Tom Woolley in the flesh," Farrah said.

I straightened up. Tom Woolley was Jack's friend, the one he was going to play tennis with this evening.

"Oh, look at his dimples." Henny smacked her lips. "I love you, you gorgeous hunk." Henny adapted well to American colloquialisms.

"Here he is playing football. He's a really good player," Farrah said. Her orange head bobbed above the books where I could see it. "These two pictures are when he was a sophomore."

"Farrah, you've got to let me have one of these pictures. You've just got to. Please Farrah, let me have just one!" Henny was pleading.

"Geez kid, you don't know how hard it was to get these pictures . . ."

She probably stole them, I thought. The cheap little thief.

"In fact, I stole them out of Woolley's locker!" Farrah confessed. I was stunned at my own clairvoyance.

"You actually stole them out of his locker?" Even Henny was impressed. "You mean Tom Woolley has actually touched these photographs? Oh precious pictures!" she swooned.

I took one Oreo from under the pillow and ate it quickly with my head low in case they stood up and looked in my direction.

"I'll tell you what, I'll lend you these two pictures, but you'll have to give them back. I don't want to give them away, but I'll lend them to you, okay?"

It was very okay with Henny, who exclaimed, "You are the very best friend I've ever had. Let's go hang them up in my room right now." Before the generous Farrah changes her witless mind.

They moved across the lawn, a collage of arms and legs.

I wiped my mouth and chin of excess chocolate crumbs.

"Wait till you see what I found today," Henny said to me as she came through the door. She hugged the photographs to her breastless chest.

"Tom Woolley."

"You heard."

"It was impossible not to."

"He's God's gift. Ask Farrah if he isn't."

I looked at Farrah with her dumb dyed hair. She was chewing gum again, her mouth rotating lazily.

"He's a real doll," she agreed.

I wondered if Farrah's taste for boys corresponded with her taste for hair stylists. She had given us a raving review of Mr. Bob and his fabulous recipe for her ghastly orange hair.

"Can I have some iced tea?" She and Henny sat down on the folding chairs. "I'm just sweating."

I nodded. She poured some into a Dixie cup.

"I'll go get some Oreos from the kitchen." Henny started to get up.

"There aren't any," I said quickly. "I looked already. Mother must have put them in Father's lunch bucket."

Henny looked doubtful. "The whole package? How come Father gets all the good stuff for his lunch bucket? That's not fair." She poured iced tea for herself.

I sat up. "Let me see the hulk."

"Hunk," Farrah corrected and giggled.

She handed me the photographs with an already practiced reverence. "Don't bend them," she said. "His name is Tom Woolley and he's president of East High School this year. That means he's a senior, Annie!" She said this as if it were supposed to mean something. "Maybe you'll have a class with him," she exclaimed. "Wouldn't that be lucky, if you did. I'm so jealous," she cried, as if my having a class with Tom Woolley was already a foregone conclusion.

I looked at the two foggy black and white snapshots. One showed a tall boy standing under a tree holding a football in one arm. The shadow of the tree fell directly across the boy's face so I could hardly decipher any features, let alone dimples.

"He's tall," I said, feeling compelled to make some comment.

"He's got huge thighs," Henny sighed.

The other snapshot was Tom Woolley's head, taken, I assume from his squinted eyes, directly in the sun. To make matters worse, the snapshot was overexposed so he looked like a bloated whitefish just taken out of water.

"These don't begin to do him justice," said Henny.

"He looks very nice, really," I said. He was no big deal.

"Well, I think he's simply beautiful, that's all." Henny

kissed Tom Woolley's picture again. "Come on Farrah, let's go paste these on the wall." She and Farrah stood up and went into the house. I waited for them to reach the kitchen and then took two more cookies out from under the pillow. I leaned on one elbow and took a bite out of both of them at once, followed by a swig of iced tea. I lay on my arm, closed my eyes, and smiled.

When my parents arrived home at nine o'clock I met them at the front door. "You've got to do something about Oma," I demanded.

Mother set her purse down on the dining-room table and asked if Oma had slept and snored on the front porch again—one of Henny's major complaints about Oma. She snored like Zeus himself, because, as Mother explained to me again, Oma has a deviated septum, an unlucky peculiarity that ran in the deWitt family.

"This is worse than a deviated septum!" I described the awful scene with Jack and his escape. "You've got to do something about her," I repeated.

"We're taking care of her the best way we know how," Mother said.

"And that's another thing. How come I'm always the one who has to sit with Oma? Why doesn't Henny have to stay home with her sometimes?"

"Did Henny come back?" Mother asked.

"She's up in our room with Farrah," I said.

Father took an apple from a bowl on the table and bit into it. "Henny only thinks of boys. Her attention span isn't long enough to take in anything else," he said. "She's too young." He chewed on the apple. My mother stood behind him, her finger following a pattern in the lace tablecloth.

"She's only a year younger than I am. That's not too young. She's sixteen. I've been watching after Oma since I was thirteen. It's not fair. I don't want to do it all the time."

My mother's lips pressed into a straight line. I was sorry I'd said anything. Mother can do that to me. Her look was so pained, and I had done it, but I couldn't apologize and I couldn't think of any more to say. I'd forgotten why I was angry. Mother's mouth . . .

"Did Jack come back later?" asked Father, changing the subject.

"No, one hosing a night is enough for him. He'll probably never come back."

My parents shared a knowing glance. "Is that his tennis racket out in the hall?" Father asked.

I nodded.

"Well, he'll have to come back and get that." He made it sound so simple.

"Why don't you just take it back to him yourself and apologize for Oma. Then you won't have to worry about what he's thinking," Mother said.

Father agreed. "I should think there's more of a risk for him to come here, especially after being chased away. Go and tell him how sorry we all are."

There was something so logical about what they both said, but I was cautious about such gestures. I didn't want anyone, especially Jack Wakefield, to think I was forward.

I decided to go.

In the bathroom I brushed my teeth and admired my tan. I pulled my hair back at the neck the way Meryl Streep did sometimes and brushed my eyebrows upward. I wondered if Jack Wakefield would notice how much I looked like a movie star.

"Where are you going?" Henny asked, standing in the doorway. Farrah had evidently gone home.

I told her. "Oma put the hose on him tonight," I explained.

Henny put her hands over her mouth and giggled. "You're kidding," she gasped. "What a riot."

60

"He was going to play tennis with your beloved Tom Woolley," I said, waiting for the explosion.

She grabbed both my shoulders. "Jack Wakefield knows Tom Woolley, that's fantastic. I mean, he can fix me up with him. He would, wouldn't he? If I asked him nicely he would, I'll bet."

"Good-bye Henny." I didn't want to hear any more of her hormonal babbling.

"Wait, I'm going with you."

"No, you're not."

"Why not?" This was a difficult question to answer, mainly because I didn't want to admit the truth: I wanted to sit with Jack Wakefield in the porch swing—the Wakefields had a swing—and have him turn to me and say, "I like your hair that way. It makes you look like Meryl Streep."

Instead I said, "Because I don't want you hyperventilating about Tom Woolley in front of Jack. That's why. You act like you're," I hesitated, "oversexed!"

I would have died of mortification if someone had labeled me "oversexed," but Henny shrugged it off and said, "Oh, don't be such a prissy prude." She waved me off with her hand and walked in front of me. "Come on, let's get over there. It's getting late."

I followed her.

As we approached the brick bungalow where Jack lived I spied the full moon glowing brightly through the overgrown blue spruce in his front yard. Henny saw it too: "Isn't the moon romantic tonight? Sure wish I were seeing it with Tom Woolley." The sound of her voice irked me.

We rang the doorbell and waited. The porch light flicked on, instantly attracting a halo of insects and June bugs. Jack stood in the doorway in fresh jeans and a blue oxford cloth shirt with the sleeves rolled up. He smelled of Old Spice aftershave.

"Is it safe?" He peeked playfully over my shoulder.

61

Henny whisked the racket out of my hand, opened the screen door and handed the racket to Jack. "We've come to apologize for Oma, and I have to talk with you for a few minutes," she said, stepping past him into the living room. She was so shovey. She seemed to be looking behind the furniture, as if Tom Woolley might be hiding there. I could hear a television in another room.

"You changed your hair," he said, holding the door open for me. He noticed, I thought. He noticed that I look like a movie star.

"She wears it like that because she thinks it makes her look like Meryl Streep," snorted Henny, sitting down on the sofa.

"No, I don't," I said much too quickly. I was positive my neck was splotched a deep purple.

"Actually, she looks like a horse with that tail hanging down her back." Henny pulled a face.

I wished I had a hand gun. I wanted to shoot her at close range.

"I like horses," I said feebly. I felt as if I were drowning in pudding.

"Want a Coke?" Jack asked.

"No, thanks. We just came to return your racket."

"Yes," said Henny, not looking at me. "I'd like some. I'm really thirsty."

"Henny, we have to go now," I said.

"We just got here," she said.

Jack studied us both. "Be back in a minute," he said and disappeared, presumably into the kitchen.

I sat on the edge of a chair by Henny and noticed a greasy stain on my white skirt. It made me feel dirty all over. I was sure wisps of greasy hair were falling around my ears. Henny looked so smug.

"Why did you have to start a fight?" I whispered furtively to her. "You're just here because you want to find out about Tom Woolley."

"So what's wrong with that?" She sat back on the sofa and folded her arms loosely as if she intended to stay there a long time.

"Why can't you keep your dumb crushes to yourself instead of involving the whole neighborhood?"

"Like you do, Meryl?" She stared coldly at me.

I hated her then. Hated her for ruining my evening, for being there at all, for being. Period. Because I couldn't think of a mean enough retort, I leaned forward and pinched her bare leg just above the knee as hard as I could, making sure to dig her skin with my fingernails.

She responded with a muffled cry and a swift, vicious kick on my shin bone. I cried "ow" and grasped my leg when Jack returned with a two-liter bottle of Coke, a stack of glasses, the kind that used to be grape jelly jars, and a bag of ginger snaps. He set it all down on the coffee table in front of Henny and me. He saw me rubbing my leg. I was trying to compose my face in spite of the throbbing limb.

"Charley horse," I groaned. "Not enough calcium." I tried to laugh. It sounded like one of my father's "heh, heh, heh's."

"You should drink only milk," Henny said.

I decided not to fight with her. I sat back in the overstuffed chair for the first time and began sipping Coke. I felt like sulking.

Jack sat on the carpet by my feet, next to the coffee table. His tanned, smooth face made me feel gloomy.

Henny leaned forward eagerly. "I met Tom Woolley tonight at the Garden Gate," she began.

I sighed an exhausted sigh.

"He was probably celebrating. He wasted me but good on the court tonight. I had to use his sister's racket. A hockey stick would have worked better," Jack said.

Henny shrieked delightedly. "Oh, he beat you."

"I'm glad to make your day," Jack muttered.

The television had stopped playing in the other room. I wondered where Jack's parents were.

"I'm just crazy about him."

"Everybody's crazy about Woolley," said Jack with his mouth full of ginger snaps. He gulped. "All the girls love his bod'. It's a gift, you know." He grinned at me. "Wait till you see him, Annie. You'll be lost to the rest of us forever."

This was a compliment. You'll be lost to *me* forever. That's what he meant, and I recognized it, but didn't know what to say. My foot swung nervously back and forth.

Henny responded for me: "Annie only likes a boy for his spiritual qualities. She loves Dan Rather," she simpered.

"I play tennis with him too," Jack said. He caught my foot and held it longer than he needed to. I began feeling better.

"Anyway," Henny started again in earnest. "I want to know if you'll fix me up with Tom Woolley. I'll just die if I can't go out with him. Will you please, Jack?" She became coy. "Pretty please?"

She was so sickening.

"Sure, but don't get your hopes up. He plays a pretty wide field."

"Do you think he'll go, though?"

"He'll go."

"Right away?"

Jack shook his head. "Can't do it until school starts," he said. "The Woolleys spend a good part of the summer on Balboa Island in California. They're leaving this weekend and won't be back until school begins. Sorry." He shrugged and leaned forward to gather up empty Coke glasses onto the tray.

"I can wait. Oh Tom, I'm coming, I'm coming." Henny danced an unrestrained waltz around the room.

Jack turned to me. "Does she talk to trees?" he asked.

"I'm sure of it," I said.

"Terrific," he said.

The next day, Jack asked me out on a date. He stopped just before lunch. His little brother Milton sat in the Chevrolet and waited for Jack. Milton's blond hair stuck straight up, and two new front teeth with scalloped edges dominated his mouth. When I stepped out onto the porch, Milton rolled the window down and yelled, "He's going to ask you out on a stupid date!"

"Shut up, Milton."

"Say no," persisted Milton. "It kills him when someone says no."

"Milton!" Jack's voice was threatening. He looked fresh and handsome in a plaid shirt.

"Jack has a girlfriend. Jack has a girlfriend."

"I was wondering if . . ." Jack stammered slightly, his hands buried deep in his pockets, but he didn't blush. I was purple, but I didn't care. I knew what was coming, thanks to Milton.

"Tell him you have to go bear hunting on Saturday night," Milton yelled.

Jack looked into my face for the first time and started to laugh helplessly. I laughed too. "Have you met my brother, Milton, soon to be hamburger?"

"He's not as bad as Oma," I said. I felt a pang of disloyalty.

"Your Oma is all right. Milton is pure turkey. Anyway, will you go out with me on Saturday night? We're going on a picnic in the mountains. We'll be going with three other couples."

"Yes, I'd like to," I said.

Milton held his nose. "You'll be sorry. He just likes girls for their bodies."

"Milton!" Jack waved a fist at him. "I'll pick you up at seven," he said, turning back to me. "I'm getting out of here before he really starts talking dirty. See you on Saturday." He practically leaped to the car.

"Did you tell her to practice up on her French kissing?" Milton asked, as Jack got into the driver's side of the car. He was still talking in a loud voice for my benefit. Jack reached over and wrenched Milton's nose, eliciting a painful squawk from his brother. When the car pulled out Milton's hands were cupped over the center of his face.

Jack. Jack Sprat could eat no fat. Jack and the beanstalk. Jack be nimble, Jack be quick, Jack jump over the candlestick. Jack Wakefield asked me out. Jack likes me, I can tell from his face. Jack-in-the-box. Jack-o'-lantern. Jack-of-all-trades. Ball and the Jacks. Jack Pot.

I called Maggie. I had to tell someone. She answered the phone on the third ring. "Aha," she said when she recognized my voice. "I was just about to call you." She was pretty excited. "Guess what?" she asked.

"I was calling you to guess what," I said.

"We're double dating on Saturday night," she squealed.

"You mean you have a date with Jack too?" I wondered which one of us he asked first.

She screeched. "You can be so foreign." She laughed on at my expense. "No, I'm going with Roger—Roger Thompson —I told you about him—he lives up the block from me. You're going with Jack. We both go to the picnic with different boys. That's a double date." She paused for air. "I don't do polygamous dating," she added.

"I thought you Mormons were all for polygamy," I said. It was a sore point with Maggie.

She groaned. "Very funny. That was a hundred years ago."

"Maggie," I hesitated. "What about Mac? Would he want you to date someone else?" Since I had known her, Maggie had talked nonstop about the marvelous Mac McBride, even read me parts of his letters. "I mean, you're practically engaged!"

"Mac won't care. Roger's just a friend." She laughed. "Actually, he's my second cousin."

I was immensely happy that Maggie was going to be at the picnic and said so.

"It'll be fun," she agreed. "You can meet Roger. You'll like Larry Johnson and Beth Knabe too. They've been going together since eighth grade. They're almost married."

"Like you and Mac," I said.

"Pretty much," she said.

"I thought there was another couple," I said. I distinctly remembered Jack mentioning three other couples.

"Oh yeah, and now the bad news: Flash and Farrah."

"Oh, not Farrah!" I was so sick of her.

"And Flash the worm. Yes, it's true. He's buddies with those guys. Don't wear your blue cotton shirt, because I'm wearing mine with my new tank top, and I don't have anything else decent to wear." She babbled on while I listened, contented, seated on the floor, pulling long threads out of the carpet.

"Do you think I should wear my glasses?" she asked.

"Can you see without them?"

"Only in soft focus. The world looks like a romantic haze." She made it sound very desirable.

"You mean you bump into things?"

"Yes."

"Wear them."

"I wish like anything I could have contact lenses now. I will look so much better. Really, I will look glorious without my glasses."

Actually Maggie always looked slightly cross-eyed without her glasses, but I didn't mention this. I just said, "It will be nice, won't it. Christmas isn't that far away."

There was a long pause in the conversation during which we both sighed heavily.

"I wish I were going with Mac," Maggie broke the silence. "It'll be fun though," she said.

"It's going to be great," I said.

In the afternoon the mailman brought a letter from Kaatje.

Edo and Froney got engaged in July while they were on vacation at the beach in Scheveningen. Kaatje couldn't remember if I'd met Froney or not before I left.

Edo was engaged! The sprinklers on the junior high school field suddenly burst on and I looked across the street at the mist above the lawn. Three shouting children had been caught by surprise at the sudden spray of water and ran laughing to the dry side of the baseball diamond. Edo was engaged and the sun was still shining.

I finished the rest of the letter warily. They planned to marry in late January when Edo finished his dissertation. Only five months away. I shouldn't be surprised, I thought. He's old enough to get married. Kaatje said she had enclosed a photograph of them. I hunted through the paper and envelope and finally found it lying at my feet. It was Edo, his dark curly hair framed the perfect face. Froney was as blond as he was dark. Her hair was thick and frizzy and hung past her shoulders. They stood on a beach, looking happy, relaxed, their arms about each other, grinning ridiculously: the future Mr. and Mrs. Edo Tefsen. I had wanted a picture of Edo ever since I could remember. Now, here it was. "I wanted to marry Edo," I said aloud and then quickly looked next door to the Spivacks' to see if anyone was sitting on their porch. No one was.

My dream of marrying Edo was an old one. I'd had it since I was twelve years old and he took Kaatje and me to see *The Nutcracker Ballet* at the Schouwburg. He sat between us. I stole short glances at him in the semi-darkness and thought then that he was the most handsome man in the world. I still thought it. After the ballet he took Kaatje and me backstage to visit my father in the lighting booth where we were allowed to push switches changing the coloring on the stage dramatically. Later, we had *poffertjes,* little dough balls deep fried in fat with powdered sugar sprinkled on top, and hot chocolate in a large tent set up next to the Dude Gracht, the main canal running through Utrecht. In recent years he had let us come with him occasionally to the movies shown on campus. I was hoping to grow up before he noticed. Beautiful Edo.

"Has the mailman come?" Henny's voice shocked me like a cold shower. She stood behind the screen door.

I nodded. "There's a card from Toby for you." I handed it to her.

"Any Dutch newspapers for Father? He's dying to read something in a language he can understand." She spotted the papers in the chair next to mine and picked them up.

"Edo Tefsen's getting married," I said, enjoying the pain of saying it aloud.

"Really?" Henny opened the front door again. "Who'd marry that flake?" The door banged shut behind her.

> Kaatje Tefsen
> Domstraat 18
> Utrecht, The Netherlands

> Kaatje, I am stunned, knocked out, and helpless in America. Edo getting married? I thought he was saving himself for Meryl Streep. Thanks for the picture. Froney looks so pretty—like the fairy queen Titania. Tell them both congratulations and wet kisses all around. Wish I could be there to celebrate.

> Love, Annie

69

P.S. Couldn't find a Ronald Reagan postcard. The bearded gentleman is Brigham Young who led the Mormon pioneers into this valley in 1847 and said, "This is the place." And it was.

I finished the postcard and reread it. Yes, it had just the right sense of *laissez faire*. So Edo's getting married, lah dee dah dee dah.

Jack's Honda sped around the corner beeping hello as he passed by. I looked up and waved. Jack is real, I thought. He's handsome and smart, and I like him. More important, he likes me back. Edo was a dream. A twelve-year-old's fantasy, a mist that rose out of an afternoon at a Christmas ballet. I resolved never to get hung up with a fantasy again. Never.

# PART 3

*August Halloween*

WHENEVER something important was about to happen in my life, like a date with Jack Wakefield, and my entire happiness depended on it, or seemed to, I got diarrhea. Mother said it was nerves.

"But what if it continues all night long?" I wailed from the bathroom. She was pressing my white jeans in her bedroom next door.

"You'll be fine," she called. That was Mother's answer for everything. "You'll be fine."

But even with diarrhea and trying on every bit of clothing I owned that looked remotely like picnic wear, I was still ready an hour before Jack arrived. He came promptly at seven o'clock. I sat on the bed, which I had pushed against the window so I could see the street better, when a covered van with THOMPSON ROOFING CONTRACTORS printed on the side in dirty gold letters pulled up in front. Two ladders hung along the van's side, a red neckerchief tacked to the ends. Jack stepped out of the back of the van along with Flash Garrett, who ran across the lawn to Farrah's house.

Henny hovered behind me, dripping from her shower, a towel wrapped around her middle, her hair sopped against her neck. Obviously, she was too curious to dry in the bathroom. We watched Jack stroll up the front walk.

"He's dressed like an undertaker," she said.

It was true. He wore an outdated black suit and tie and even carried a black bowler under his arm.

"It looks like you're going to a costume party," she said. "I thought you were going on a picnic."

I ran down the stairs. "I thought so too," I called back.

Father had answered the front door before the door bell even rang, much to my mortification. Our whole family must have been watching at windows waiting for Jack to arrive. I wondered where Oma was. Out of the way, I hoped.

"Howdy," I could hear my father say too loudly. He liked cowboy talk, and tried to imitate the whole cast of *Hee Haw* on television.

"Howdy, Mr. Sehlmeier," Jack returned. They shook hands.

"Hi," I said, squeezing into the vestibule. "I thought we were going on a picnic." My nose wrinkled involuntarily. Jack had the faint odor of moth balls about him.

"We are," Jack said, his face peculiarly solemn. "After."

I waited for him to finish, but he didn't say any more.

"After what?" I asked.

"After we help Roger's dad. We have to do it before the picnic. Don't worry," he said, "It won't take long. Roger's dad said we should wear these suits."

"You are beautiful in the suit," my father said to Jack. We were still squeezed into the vestibule, but I didn't want to move into the living room and give Father an opportunity for winded conversations à la Minnie Pearl. "Very beautiful," continued my father. I wished he would shut up.

"I'm ready," I said. "Are you sure you don't want me to change into sequins or something?"

"Yeah!—No," said Jack, opening the front door and nodding good-bye to my father. "Have you met the Reverend Moon?

"Does he go to the high school too?"

Jack laughed. "No, it's the van. The van is called the Reverend Moon. You know, the Moonies. We've never had a bad time in this van," he said and opened the back door.

"Hello," called Maggie from the front seat. A freckled boy with rust-colored, curly hair sat behind the wheel. Another boy and girl sat on the floor of the van leaning against the wall. The front seats were evidently the only seats in the van.

"This is our place." Jack pushed me opposite the boy and girl. "This is Annie Sehlmeier," Jack said as we leaned back. "That's Larry Johnson and Beth Knabe," he nodded at the couple sitting across from us. She leaned against him, his arm around her. They looked almost married.

"That's Roger, driving the Moon, and you know Maggie, of course." There was a chorus of "hi," and "glad to meet ya," followed by nervous laughter in general and my own specifically.

All of the boys wore baggy black suits and ties, including Flash Garrett, who appeared at the back door, and let Farrah in.

The greetings were repeated. Farrah sat on the other side of me and squeezed my hand. "Kid, you look darling," she said, as if she were surprised. She blinked significantly at Jack. Her blazing head bobbed with meaning. She wore an orange blouse and orange slacks the same shade as her hair and a pair of orange, heart-shaped sunglasses. She looked like a creepy pumpkin.

"You guys look like death warmed over," Farrah said. "Did you all attend the same truck sale?"

"You and Flash look like Halloween," said Larry. "So you fit right in."

Farrah looked at herself and at Flash. "I guess the colors

75

are right," she said. "Dracula," she growled at Flash and gave him a wet kiss right on the lips. I couldn't believe it.

"Oh, what a lovely throat," croaked Flash and bit Farrah's neck right by her ear. Farrah loved it.

"Hey you guys, hold off for a while, will ya!" Roger seemed irritated. The truck jolted forward. Roger made an illegal U-turn on 8th South and headed toward the canyon. "Wait until we get Uncle Harrison taken care of, can't you?"

"I haven't forgotten, stay cool," Flash said. He leaned against the truck wall and Farrah leaned into him. I noticed he wore white socks with his black suit, which supported my whole theory about Flash: tacky, tacky, tacky.

"Who is this Harrison guy?" Beth asked.

"A distant uncle of Roger's. He needs some help and Mr. Thompson asked us to do it," Larry explained.

"Look, let's not talk about it at all," Roger shot back. Boy, was he nervous. "Let's just go do it and get on with this picnic."

Maggie glanced at me, pushing her glasses back off her nose, and shrugged. "I've never heard of this Harrison guy," she said.

Roger snapped. "He's my father's uncle. You're not related to him at all."

He swerved the truck onto a frontage road that ran parallel with the highway and then separated, hugging Flat Top Mountain and cutting the sun from our view. The back of the truck grew dark. I shifted my position because one leg was going to sleep. My foot hit some shovels that lay down the center of the truck. I hadn't noticed them until they clanged together. Beth noticed them too. She mouthed the word "weird" to me and shrugged. I smiled. I liked her. Jack took my hand and held it in his lap as if we'd held hands all our lives. "We're almost there, I think," he said.

Roger heard him. "I hope I haven't missed that dirt road. Dad said it was a couple of miles past the old mill."

"There, to the left," Maggie pointed.

"Yeah, that's it. Thanks," he said. He turned left again onto a dirt road, nothing more than a wide trail, really. The dust lifted on either side of the van.

"Don't you have a cabin up here somewhere?" Maggie asked him.

"It's further up the road, around the other side of the mountain from here," Roger said.

The van bumped and swayed along the spiraling upward trail. The shovels clattered against each other. The ladders hanging on the outside of the van shifted and grated against the wall. One large bump rocked us all off our seats.

That's when I noticed the rifle behind Larry's back. It was hidden in canvas, which had become partially unwrapped with the rocky ride. Larry noticed it immediately and covered it up. He held his hand on the canvas so it wouldn't come loose again. He watched my face, smiled blandly at me and then looked away. He didn't want me to see it. I was sure of that. It occurred to me that I didn't know any of these people very well, and that my parents didn't have the foggiest notion of where I was. I could be kidnapped. Killed, even.

"This ride has bruised places on my body that aren't generally bruised," Jack whispered.

"Me too," I said.

I trusted Jack. He wasn't the guerrilla type. None of them was, except Larry. Larry was some kind of psycho, perhaps, and had brought the gun without anyone else knowing.

"I'm starving," Farrah cried. "Geez, when will we get there? And where are we?" Whine, whine, whine.

"Flat Top Mountain. We're here," Roger called back. He swerved the van into a clearing between two clumps of towering pine trees and shut off the engine. "We're here," he said again. "Everybody out. Grab the shovels, Jack." He climbed out of the truck and ran around to the other side to help Maggie out, but she was already standing alongside the open door.

"This is a graveyard," she said.

The rest of us climbed out of the back of the van. Jack and Flash carried the four shovels while Psycho Larry carried the canvas-wrapped weapon.

The graveyard was a small clearing in a grove of old pine trees at the base of the mountain.

"What is this?" Beth asked, her arms folded tightly across her abdomen. "I mean, *really.*"

"It's creepy," said Farrah.

"Jack?" I asked.

"Okay, ladies, there's no cause for concern." Roger raised his arms as if he were calming a revival tent of people.

"Explain," Maggie demanded.

"This is an old Thompson family graveyard. There used to be a settlement here about sixty years ago, but because of rock slides, they moved it around the mountain—where our cabin is now." He watched Maggie. "My great Uncle Harrison Thompson is buried," he walked a few steps, "here," he finished. He stood next to a decrepit black wooden marker. Harrison Thompson's name was barely visible on it. The grave marker sat, tilted, off balance on the burial mound. A small whirlwind lifted and swirled the dried needles around Roger's feet.

"My father asked if we would dig him up," he said.

"That's sick." We girls all spoke at once.

"It sounds unanimous," Jack said lifting eyebrows at Roger.

"Now wait," Roger lifted his arms again. I was sure he was destined to be a preacher or one of those Mormon bishops or something. "Hear me out. It's not a joke." Certainly his face was serious enough, although he looked goofy under the black felt bowler. All the boys wore them now. Jack looked pretty solemn himself. And handsome.

78

"My father," continued Roger, "has been working on his genealogy—you know—family history and that kind of stuff, and he found a document, sort of like a will, written by Harrison Thompson that says he wants to be buried under his own house."

"There's no house here," Maggie said.

"Exactly," Roger shifted feet. "But there used to be. Our cabin was Harrison's house. After he died it was moved to the other side of the mountain because of the rock slides. See how his grave is removed from the rest of the graveyard? He was buried under his house. My dad, after he found this will in Harrison's own handwriting, wants to . . ."

"Bury him under his own house again," Maggie finished.

"That's right," Roger said. "All he wants us to do is dig him up and then he and Uncle Fay will take him to the cabin tomorrow."

"Uncle *Fay?*" Sounds like you're making it all up," said Beth.

"Looks like it too. You guys in your black suits and bowlers." Maggie popped her lips on "bowlers."

"We didn't want to wear these stupid suits," Jack said, "but Roger's dad has this incredible respect for his dead ancestors."

"Not to mention Uncle Fay," Roger interrupted.

"Look, maybe we should have our picnic now," suggested Larry. He shifted the canvas load to his other arm. "Then after we take the girls home we'll come back and do it. It'll be harder in pitch black, but we don't need the flack either."

"Good idea, I'm starved," Farrah said.

"Oh go ahead. We can wait," Beth said. "Can't we?" She turned to me and Maggie. We both nodded.

"I'm starving," whined Farrah.

"It won't take long," Jack said. "Go ahead, Roger."

Everybody automatically turned to Roger. For a moment I thought he was going to dig up the grave all by himself.

79

"Will you all stand in a circle around the grave while I say a prayer?"

"You're going to pray? Now?" Farrah asked. "What for?"

"It's common to have dedicatory prayers when people are buried."

"But you are unburying," Beth pointed out.

"My father asked that we . . ."

"Okay, okay," Beth gestured for him to get on with it.

"If this is a joke, you're blaspheming!" Maggie pointed her finger at Roger. "All of you are."

"This is no joke," Roger said, his face taut. The boys all looked pretty grim, and a little hurt, even, that we might not believe them.

"You don't have to participate in the prayer, Maggie." He bowed his head and began praying aloud: "Father in Heaven, as we prepare to dig up the grave of my great uncle Harrison Thompson, we ask to invoke thy spirit on this serious undertaking."

I felt like a fool. All of us standing there with bowed heads. I'd never heard anyone my age pray before. It sounded downright bizarre to me, but I knew Mormons prayed about everything, and who was I to take objection to that? Still I felt foolish with my head bowed under Flat Top Mountain.

Finally Roger finished the prayer.

"Get the gun and stand out by the gate," he said to Larry after the amen.

"I've got it here." Larry patted the canvas.

"You've got a gun?" Beth was incredulous. "Why do you need a gun?"

"Just to warn us if someone is coming," Roger said.

"Isn't this your family graveyard?" I asked. "Are you breaking the law?"

"It is the family graveyard, but people might not understand a bunch of kids digging around in it." Larry took the rifle out of the canvas and walked to a broken down gate where the road curved suddenly.

"This is going to take all night," moaned Farrah.

I sat on a huge rock. Maggie sat next to me.

"Can you believe this?" She said to me. "I'll bet they never find a thing and when they've dug a hole the size of Salt Lake County, they'll yell 'April Fools' or some dumb thing."

Beth sat on the ground by our feet. "I don't know," she said. "Roger was sure nervous on the way up here."

Roger used a pickax to loosen the dirt while the other two boys scooped it away with the shovels. Larry sat on the fence, a hazy figure in the twilight, his gun pointed toward the sky. Jack dug in a hole about one foot deep, perspiration beaded on his forehead. "One down, and five to go," he said. "I wouldn't want to do this for a living." Flash pulled a lantern out of the van, lit it, and set it next to the growing hole. "It's going to be dark soon," he said. The boys continued digging, their faces serious as church. We girls sprawled on and beside our rock of refuge, made faces at one another, and swatted mosquitoes.

"I hit something!" Roger yelled.

"Me too," followed Jack.

We girls leaned forward. The boys scooped dirt with their hands.

"There really is a body then," breathed Maggie. "How gross."

Larry came running from his guard duty, rifle in hand. "Did you find it?" he asked, breathless.

"Yeah, give us a hand," Jack said. He was digging around the end of the coffin. When the box was free, Roger and Jack lifted up one end with Flash and Larry at the other, and set the coffin on the pine-covered ground, right at our feet. Beth withdrew a Capezio'd foot and tucked it safely under her legs. The coffin was a simple black wooden box, half rotted from the moisture. Dirt was clotted onto the sides, and I thought I saw some slugs glistening in the lantern light. I really hate the look of slugs.

"Let's fill up the hole," Roger said.

The boys stamped the dirt on the filled-up hole and Jack and Flash swept pine needles onto it with their hands. "Good work," Roger said, and started shaking hands with Larry and then with Jack and Flash. For the first time that night they all laughed a little, with relief, I think. They hit each other on the back and shook hands all over again, repeating, "good work" as they did so.

We hung around while they put their jackets on and readjusted their ties.

After the boys were neat again, and they had returned the shovels and the rifle, much to my relief, back to the van, we all stood around Harrison Thompson's coffin silently, the boys holding their hats in their hands. I wondered if we were about to pray again, but no one spoke. Maybe we were praying silently, everyone but me, that is; but I looked at Maggie who stared back over the rims of her glasses and shrugged at me. We waited.

"Let's open it up," said Flash.

"No!" All the girls said it at the same time.

"Don't you dare!" Farrah screamed.

"I think it's the opportunity of a lifetime," said Larry placidly. "I mean, unless we go to med school, we'll never have an opportunity to see a cadaver." Larry was back into being psycho as far as I was concerned.

"He's been dead over sixty years," Beth screeched. "Are you nuts?"

"Aren't you just a little curious?" Jack asked.

"Not enough to open it," said Maggie.

"Not at all," I said. "It's probably filled with slugs." I couldn't help but shiver.

"Or worse," said Beth.

"Look, let's open it up. You don't have to look at all," Roger said. "You can go sit in the van."

"I don't need to sit in the van," said Maggie.

"You're all perverts," Beth said.

But they were softening. I could tell. They were playing games. They were going to allow it. Something tightened in my chest. Oh, I knew Harrison Thompson was indifferent to the whole thing and had been dead sixty odd years, but I wasn't going to be a part of it, and I said so: "I'm going home," I said evenly, and began walking as fast as I could down the gravel road toward the gate. There was enough moonlight to see me all the way home.

"Annie, don't!" Jack's voice trailed behind me. I kept walking. No one, not even Jack Wakefield, could make me stay and look at some poor decayed corpse.

"Annie," Jack stood beside me, gripping my arm. "Don't go," he said. He had black dirt smudged across his cheek.

"It's not right," I whispered. "I don't want to be a part of it."

"It's stupid, really stupid, I guess."

"Yes, it is." My face felt roaring hot again.

"Trust me for five minutes? It's not as bad as it seems. Really, it's not." I looked around his shoulder down the roadway and tried to think. He smelled of Old Spice and mothballs.

"If you still want to leave in five minutes, I'll walk home with you." He held up one hand, his fingers spread out. "Just five minutes."

"No more than five," I said.

"Good." He grinned, obviously relieved. He grasped my hand and led me back to the group. "It's okay," Jack said.

"For five minutes, anyway," I corrected.

"Open it up." Flash's foot twisted, knocking the lantern over. The light went out.

"Damn, I can't get it lit," he said, hovering over the Coleman.

"Good, we'll see less of him," Maggie said.

Overhead, on either side, the pines moaned with the canyon wind. We all stood for a few seconds, our eyes adjusting to the moonlight.

Roger inserted the crowbar again. "It's loose," he said. "We can take the top off." He and Larry each held to an end. "Move it to the right," said Roger. They shifted the top and when they did, we heard a rattle, like the rattling of bones, and suddenly this thing, this skeleton, leaped straight into the air and landed at Farrah's feet.

We all screamed. I screamed bloody murder. Maggie's glasses fell to the ground when she tried to cover her face. Beth screamed in staccato, as if she couldn't catch her breath.

I mean, it just popped out of the box like those snakes in the phony candy tins. Farrah jumped hysterically up and down and up and down, screeching and beating on Flash, and couldn't stop even when the rest of us began laughing. The skeleton was plastic, a toy with empty tin cans tied to its limbs to make it rattle more.

Jack leaned over. "It's Milton's," he laughed.

"It figures," I said. I swatted him with relief.

"Poor Uncle Harrison." Roger picked up the plastic skeleton.

"Plastic spine," Maggie observed, putting her glasses on again. "Runs in the family, I'll bet."

"There's more in here!" Larry said.

"Don't let it pop out," said Beth. "I couldn't stand it."

"It's probably Roger's spineless aunt." Maggie was making the skeleton tap dance. "Or his Uncle Fay!"

"It's dinner," said Jack. He and Larry lifted out two Styrofoam boxes and a cold drink jug. We girls were speechless for the first time.

Roger listed the food as he pulled off the lids: "Fried

chicken, potato salad, potato chips, grapes and chocolate cake."

"You guys buried all of this today?" Beth was impressed.

"This afternoon. We haven't done anything but dig all day," Jack said. "The most difficult dinner date I've ever had, especially since I almost lost my date in the process."

Roger pulled a checkered cloth out of one of the boxes and spread it on the ground. Flash relit the lantern, "Why it does work," he said with exaggeration. "A miracle."

"Sit down, ladies, we will serve you." Jack bowed and handed out paper plates to each of us, while Larry poured punch. We girls sat at the edge of the checkered cloth, hesitant at first to begin, tittering over each delicacy dished onto our plates and finally inhaling every morsel.

"I want to know where you got the ugly black suits," Maggie said.

"The D.I.," Roger said. "Deseret Industries," he explained to me. "It's all used stuff. We had to go to three different stores, including the one in Provo."

"Mine cost two whole bucks." Jack took another drumstick out of the basket.

"You got cheated," Maggie said. "You all look terrible."

"Oh really?" Larry carefully smoothed a lapel. "I was planning to be married in this suit." He made a face at Beth.

"Over my dead body," Beth said with her mouth full.

"Then we'll have to bury *you* in it," Larry said. They began throwing food at each other.

"Don't!" Farrah shrieked. "Don't fight with the food—I'm not finished eating yet."

Flash placed the whole basket of chicken into her lap and then handed her the entire chocolate cake. "Will this be enough?" he asked.

After dinner Roger turned on the van lights and the radio, and we danced to country western music. Jack insisted that they teach me to square dance as part of my western education: "They forced us to learn it in grade school. Why should you get off scot-free?" he said. Maggie called out directions for a Virginia reel which we danced to a Willie Nelson song. The boys hee-hawed their way through it. I didn't have the least idea of what the dance was about, but by watching the others, and their shoving me or pulling me into place, I got through it. Then Flash changed the station to something with slow music at Farrah's request and turned off the lights.

Jack and I danced, our bodies and faces touching. The pine needles crunched beneath our feet while an August moon poured silver slivers of light onto our mountain dance floor. Lionel Richie's voice crooned, accompanied by the rustling pines. I felt warm, calm, and safe in Jack's arms. I was sure I would never want another thing in my whole entire life.

# PART 4

## *Obsessions*

THE week before school began, Maggie took me in to meet the Senior Choir Director, Miss Boyle. Miss Boyle sat working at her desk. She was about forty-five years old. Her hair was strawberry blond, tightly permanented, and her nose seemed longer than it actually was because of her thin lips.

She rose when she saw Maggie, grasped her arm warmly, and gave her a half hug. "My favorite soprano-accompanist," she said.

"I've brought you an another accompanist," she beamed. "She sings alto." Maggie explained how I was new and "very musical" and just *had* to be in the choir.

"I don't really need another alto," Miss Boyle said.

"No one ever needs another alto," I agreed.

She nodded her head and gave me a little half smile.

"You could use another accompanist, though," Maggie argued.

Miss Boyle walked into the choir room and sat down at the piano, where she played various scales. "Sing this back to me," she said to me. I followed her directions, and sang several scales.

"You're not an alto, you're a bass," she muttered, smiling. "You have a very low range."

She had me sight-read. "Nice," she said.

"Wait until you hear her play the piano!" Maggie was not about to allow Miss Boyle to keep me out of the choir.

I played the same ballade I had played for Maggie and her parents. Miss Boyle closed her eyes through part of it.

"Lovely," she said, when I was finished. She explained that the choir was mainly an a-cappella choir but that some pieces did have piano accompaniment. She laid a piece of sheet music in front of me, a wild rendition of Luther's "A Mighty Fortress is Our God," asked me to sight-read it for her. I worked through it with minor errors, following Miss Boyle's conducting arm. Maggie bit her nails.

"Third alto," said Miss Boyle when I finished. "That means you sing with the tenors occasionally. You can trade off with Maggie on the accompanying."

"Terrific!" Maggie jumped out of her seat.

In the office I received a list of my classes and their locations. Maggie was slightly piqued that we only had choir together. "I think Jack has the same homeroom as you," she said. "I'm almost sure he has Mr. Crow first." She leaned her head close to mine. "So you won't get any work done in English." She giggled.

> Kaatje Tefsen
> Domstraat 18
> Utrecht, The Netherlands

Kaatje, the girls here wear bras! I can't believe it. Just like old women. It's so disgusting. Maggie and I practically had a fight over it today. She took me up to the high school to try out for Senior Choir and to pick up my program.

I told Maggie I wasn't going to take gym. She said I couldn't graduate without it. It was a requirement. I repeated that it was stupid. They didn't even have gym in Holland, I told her.

"You just don't want to wear a bra," she said out of the blue. "And in gym you'll have to."

"What has wearing a bra got to do with anything? I've never worn a bra in my entire life," I told her.

And then she said, "So I've noticed. You're going to have to wear one in gym or else you'll be the laughingstock of the class. You have to change your clothes and everyone will notice that you don't wear one—you'll be the only one without a bra." That's what she said to me. It was pretty hostile too.

"Forget it! Do you wear a bra?" I asked her. I really couldn't believe I was having this conversation.

"Of course," she said. "Everyone I know does. I was going to speak to you about it earlier after Beth said something to me."

I thought I had just been thrown back to the Victorian era. I just stared at her in amazement. "I am not going to wear a bra ever," I said as emphatically as I could.

"My mother told me to tell you too." She lowered her voice slightly to tell me this. "She says you look great without one, but she's afraid you might get teased since it's out of the ordinary here. She said you could get away with it easily if we lived on one of the coasts, but not here. Not yet."

Maggie's mother is just gorgeous, Kaatje. If she would say something like that, well then, I knew I had reason to worry.

"Anyone else have anything to say about my need for

91

more underwear? Flash Garrett? Jack? The postman?" I asked Maggie.

And then, Kaatje, I let her take me out to ZCMI in the Cottonwood Mall to buy a bra. When you come to visit me next summer, I will insist that you wear one too, only a big padded one, the size of Dolly Parton. You won't be able to see your feet!

Is Edo really getting married?

I miss you.

> Kiss, kiss, kiss,
> Annie

I dreamed I slept through the alarm by three hours on the first day of school. Henny had left long before. I tried to dress quickly, but none of my clothes seemed to fit, and the new shoes I had bought turned into blue rabbit slippers when I put them on. Mother was unconcerned. She sharpened yellow pencils in the faucet of the kitchen sink. "You will have to take Oma with you," she said, not looking at me. "It's your turn to take care of her." Oma and I were pulled by a tow rope up 8th South to reach the school. Oma let go of the rope just as we were almost there and held on to my slacks instead, tearing off the whole backside, so that my behind was absolutely bare. Both of us slid down 8th South but scrambled back up on all fours. I was aware of my bare backside. Inside the school I hugged the walls so that no one could see that half my clothes were missing. Oma stayed close by. She repeatedly pinched my bottom, even when I asked her to stop. I found Mr. Crow's room and opened the door. Thirty faces stared up at me. Each person wore the same red jacket as mine. Oma announced in perfect English: "Annie isn't wearing any underpants!"

Actually, I was up in plenty of time. I brushed my hair like Meryl Streep's in the Stars calendar, parted at the side.

"Today is the day," Henny sang. She searched for shoes under the bed. "Today is the day I get to see Tom Woolley again. Oh joy." She lightly kissed the snapshots above her bed.

She irritated me to death. My hair was too curly.

"Will you shut up about Tom Woolley all the time," I seethed.

She made a face at me. "Tom Woolley, Tom Woolley, Tom Woolley, Tom Woolley, Tom Woolley, Tom Woolley, Tom Woolley," she repeated.

I knew I would despise Tom Woolley.

Jack was the first person I saw when I entered Mr. Crow's advanced placement English class. He sat midway back in the center of the classroom and waved at me to sit next to him. He looked wonderful in khaki pants and a plaid shirt. Beth Knabe sat directly in front of him.

"How have you been?" Beth asked.

"Are you nervous?" Jack asked.

"Fine, a little," I said, answering both of them. "My English isn't good enough for an English-English class, I'm afraid. I'm not sure I belong in advanced placement." My hands were a little cold.

"You'll be fine," Jack said. "Really." He smiled. He looked a little nervous himself. Roger walked in and sat near the front. He nodded and waved at us.

The class was filling up fast now. Mr. Crow's name was written on the blackboard in the front, although he wasn't there yet. A wall of windows with brown canvas blinds was off to the left. Mr. Crow's desk stood at the side of the room with a computer on top and a wire basket filled with files.

When I turned my head back, *he* was standing in the doorway. He stood well over six feet tall, his hair thick and dark and curly; his violet eyes were rimmed with black lashes, and when he smiled, his teeth gleamed in perfect alignment. Edo, I thought. He nodded at someone. At Jack! His lips. His dimples. His lips. Something inside of me crumpled, my stomach, perhaps. He came toward us. I didn't care if I stared. I wouldn't look away from that perfect face. The likeness to Edo was uncanny.

He slapped Jack on the back, "Jack, you jerk." He grinned. "Improve your game yet?" He turned to me. "Who is this?" he asked, leaning over my desk. His breath was perfumed with aftershave lotion, a sensuous scent I couldn't identify. The fragrance was dizzying. I wondered if he gargled with it.

"This is Annie Sehlmeier," Jack said. "This is Tom Woolley."

If I had been a cartoon drawing, I would have been surrounded with little fat hearts with BOING printed in each one.

"Hi," I said.

"Jack," Tom Woolley said, his face right next to mine, "you didn't tell me that she looked exactly like Meryl Streep."

"Oh brother," Jack snorted. "Watch out, Annie, he's a smooth one."

The smooth one sat down in the seat directly in front of me. His magnificent odor permeated my space.

He turned. "Call me Woolley," he said. "Nobody calls me Tom."

"Except his mother," giggled Beth.

"Bethie, please." He pretended to pout. "You live in Jack's neighborhood, right?" he asked, turning around.

"On 8th South." I nodded.

"Her family moved from Holland this summer," Jack said.

"Oh yes, I remember. You told me. You weren't very complete with your information, though." He winked at me. "I'm Dutch too, you know."

"Are you kidding me?" Jack turned away covering his face with his hand.

"I am," Woolley insisted a little louder for Jack's benefit. "I'm one quarter Dutch. My maternal grandmother came from Holland. Johanna Van Fleet was her name."

"That's Dutch all right," I said.

"I can even speak a little Dutch," Woolley said.

Jack pretended to gag.

*"Dag,"* Woolley said as if he'd just recited *The Iliad* in Greek.

Jack guffawed. "I know more Dutch than that!" he said.

"Yeah, but my accent's perfect, isn't it Annie?"

"It's not bad." I laughed.

Woolley's elbow rested on my desk. I wanted to reach out and rub the palm of my hand up and down his arm, under his shirt sleeve. I felt insanely idiotic and happy.

The bell rang and Mr. Crow appeared, shutting the door behind him. He was a thin, rather rigid-looking man, whose hair was parted too close to the center of his head, making him look old-fashioned. He wore a tweed jacket with a knit tie. His voice droned low. We would study six weeks of mythology and then read Macbeth, which would take us to Christmas. I tried to watch him, but my eyes wanted to fix themselves on Woolley's neck, his hairline.

Mr. Crow checked the roll and then introduced us to some mythological figures we would be discussing in the next several weeks, writing their names on the blackboard as he discussed them: Zeus and Hera. Athena, Poseidon, and Apollo, the most beautiful of the gods.

He's sitting in front of me, I thought.

"Apollo was fed nectar and ambrosia by Themis," Mr. Crow's voice droned on.

That's why his breath is so sweet. I leaned forward to get a better whiff.

Mr. Crow spoke of other gods after Apollo, but I didn't hear or read their names on the board. I hovered above the desk, millions of little flapping wings keeping me aloft, and admired my own newly found god: Apollo Woolley.

After class I walked upstairs to choir between Woolley and Jack. Woolley never spoke without leaning his head close to mine, as if he whispered a secret only for me to hear. Jack looked amused and skeptical.

Maggie waited at Miss Boyle's door.

"Magnificent Maggie," Woolley said. He put out his hand for her to shake and held it.

"Woolley, Woolley, Woolley," Maggie returned. She removed her hand playfully from his grasp.

"What do you hear from Mac?"

"He's in Florence right now. School doesn't start for another couple of weeks for him. "You've met god's gift, I see," she said to me.

Jack opened the door. "She has, and she's still walking a straight line." Jack laughed.

I like you, Jack. Something crazy is happening to me today, but I still like you.

"You overestimate my influence," Woolley said rubbing his chest with one hand. He gazed about the choir room.

"Only you do that," Maggie said. "How was first period?" she asked me.

"Pretty good," I said. "Beth is in there too."

Jack and Woolley moved into the bass section.

"We'd better sit down," Maggie said. "We begin right at the bell. Miss Boyle trained us in junior choir last year." She pushed me toward the alto section. Woolley winked at me as I crossed in front of the basses.

The bell rang. The choir began humming.

"We're supposed to try humming an A note," Beth whispered, when she saw me looking quizzically about. She sat next to me.

"We're flat," I said.

"We're always flat," she giggled. "Sit forward, or she'll lower your grade."

I straightened my back and hummed a flat A.

Miss Boyle came out of her office and struck an A note on the piano. The choir groaned.

"It's been a long summer. Let's warm up," she said. We sang scales on ooh and aah. Miss Boyle was a perfectionist. I was glad to be in her choir.

Third period was advanced algebra, where I literally panicked when I opened the text. Some of the problems looked familiar, but the instructions were written with vocabulary totally foreign to me. What was an integer? I would have to translate the entire book into Dutch before understanding the instructions. It would take forever, and that didn't count working the problems. I could hardly breathe just thinking about it. Mr. Dayton, the teacher, introduced me to the class as a foreign exchange student, and I didn't bother to correct him. I'm going to fail school, I thought. I'm going to fail.

It was almost a relief to have gym the next period. We changed into blue shorts and white blouses in the locker room. Maggie was right. Everyone, but everyone, wore a bra. Including me. Ms. Needham, the gym teacher, was a masculine-looking woman with short hair and unusually muscular limbs. It reminded me of an ad I'd seen for a movie called *Pumping Iron* with these body-building, sexy females posed in various states of flexing. There was nothing sexy about Ms. Needham though. She was shaped like a cube. We followed her outside to the track surrounding the football field and ran two laps. I ran alongside a girl named Denise Beckstrand, kind of a New Waver—her hair stuck up in an unusually strange way in the front. It reminded me of Woody

Woodpecker. She had met Henny earlier in the day and asked me if I was her sister. She said we looked exactly alike. Great, I thought: Tweedledee and Tweedledum. The rest of the hour was spent playing some kind of speedball followed by the usual communal shower.

Maggie met me in front of the gym and took me down to the cafeteria, which was in the basement. Beth and another girl, Nedra Stone, had saved places for us. Nedra was the most gorgeous girl I'd ever seen.

After lunch is not a good time to have physiology. I sat near the back of "the pit" where the gray-headed Ms. Humphries gave her lectures so I was looking down at her, which made it almost impossible to keep my eyes open. I was so incredibly sleepy. Larry Johnson sat next to me, his elbow propped on the desk, head resting on his fist trying to look awake, but he was dozing. In mid-sentence, Ms. Humphries threw a piece of chalk, hitting Larry square on the top of his head. "Bullseye!" she cried, glaring into Larry's startled face. "I don't want anyone sleeping in my class," she said, her eyes seemed to cover the whole room at once. "Do you understand?" She was back to Larry again.

"Yes ma'am," he said, straightening his sagging body as best as he could. "It's going to be a long year," he muttered to me when Ms. Humphries's back was turned. I pinched my arms ruthlessly to keep from dozing off. It was going to be a long hour.

Of all the teachers, I liked Mr. Benson in my U.S. history class the best. He was probably in his late thirties, although it was hard to tell because he was a little overweight and he was graying at the temples. His face was square and friendly, and he spent the whole hour talking about the value of time, how quickly it passed, how it seemed like only yesterday that he had graduated from high school himself. It was time for us to decide what we were going to do and be. He was especially concerned with our "being," and quoted Erich Fromm extensively. Sometimes he would pause and stare out the window in a meaningful sort of way and then gaze at us as if words were not enough to communicate the message he had to deliver. He stopped exactly with the bell and smiled us all out of the classroom. A girl whose name I didn't know yet whispered to me on the way out the door that her older sister had told her that Benson gave that same speech at the beginning of every term. I nodded. Maybe a little corny, but I liked it.

My locker was located on the second floor around the corner from Mr. Benson's classroom and I had to pass a stairwell to get to it. *"Dag,* Annie Sehlmeier!" I looked up and saw Woolley standing at the top of the stairs with the beautiful Nedra Stone. "See you tomorrow." He waved. Nedra smiled at me and then at Woolley.

*"Tot ziens,"* I said.

When I got home from school, I ran upstairs immediately. "Be back in a minute," I said to my mother, practically knocking her down in the kitchen. I kneeled on Henny's unmade bed and gazed at the two photos of Tom Woolley taped to the wall. He looked so beautiful, so perfect in them. Why hadn't I noticed it before? I touched each picture and knew I wanted them for my very own.

"How can you do this to me?" I asked the photos. "How can you make me feel this way? I feel so crazy." Even as I said this, I realized I was speaking aloud to a photograph. I pulled the picture of Edo and Froney out of my desk and held it up to Woolley's face. They looked so much alike, only Woolley had those astonishing violet eyes, while Edo's were a deep brown.

I wanted to dance, to sing and shriek his name. I love Tom Woolley. I love Tom Woolley. I wanted to act just like Henny. A sobering thought.

The back door slammed and Henny's high-pitched shriek

carried up into the bedroom. Mother mumbled some kind of reprimand I couldn't hear.

"I can't help it," Henny screeched. "Tom Woolley is taking me out on Saturday night. Me. Can you believe it? Me. To the movies. Me and Tom Woolley."

I crossed the room and sat on my bed. She was so lucky. So incredibly lucky. I heard her thump up the stairs. Quickly I began changing my clothes.

"Annie." Her face shone like some celestial beacon. "I'm going out with Tom Woolley. Jack fixed me up." She crossed over the taped line and squeezed me around the shoulders.

"Isn't that incredible? Isn't it fantastic?" She oozed enthusiasm.

So Jack had kept his word. I felt my shoulders slump.

"Great," I said. My notebook was opened to a page of doodled hearts with "Apollo" written several times along one side: the sum total of my English notes.

"Woolley sits in front of me in first period," I said. "He's also in my choir class. He seems quite nice," I added.

"Nice? Nice?" Henny threw her arms up. "Annie, didn't you notice how gorgeous he is? He's perfect."

I wanted to say, "Did I notice? I'm wild about him. I've had palpitations all day because of him. I adore him. I love him." Instead, I said, "He reminds me of Edo Tefsen."

"Oh spare me," she said. She leaned across her bed and kissed Woolley's photo and let out another piercing scream.

"Get ahold of yourself," I said. I could have been talking to myself.

"Impossible." She laughed. She danced and leaped about the room.

For the rest of the week I sat behind Woolley and weighed the risks of leaning forward and kissing the back of his smooth neck. The smell of his aftershave hovered under my nose, made me dizzy. What exactly would the rest of my life be like if I kissed that stunning neck? Planted both lips on his skin and left them there like some sucking leech? I pictured newspaper headlines, GIRL'S LIPS STUCK TO BOY'S NECK. Once I craned my head forward, and Jack leaned over to ask if I had a headache.

Jack was the confusing thing. I still thought him attractive. I still wanted to be around him. He smiled at me, and a warm dizziness took hold of me.

I am crazed, I thought. Soon, I will love every boy in this school. I'll walk with my tongue extended like a sloppy dog and drool over their looks, their smiles, their poetic greetings: "Hi ya, Annie."

Kaatje Tefsen
Domstraat 18
Utrecht, The Netherlands
Saturday morning

Kaatje, my first week of school has been terrifying and exhausting. I like my classes except for gym, and even it isn't all that bad except I hate to change my clothes and shower in the middle of the day. The worst of it is the written homework. I have cried at least once every single night this week. I had to write a simple paper for English about a childhood memory. I wrote about the time Edo took us to the *Nutcracker* ballet at Christmastime, and he wore that bright red wool tie with his gray sports coat, remember? If I could have written it in Dutch, it would have taken no longer than an hour. I worked on it *four* hours, looking up every other word for spelling. It was just ghastly. And the words I need translated for algebra aren't even in my dictionary half the time. All my friends are planning to go to the University of Utah next year. What if I can't get in? I stay up past midnight each night just doing my homework, and I'm so tired.

Even Dr. Wirthlin noticed I looked tired. Tante Geert took me in to him yesterday afternoon after school because of the nosebleeds. He said if they didn't stop I'd have to have my nose cauterized, which means he burns off the little blood vessels in my nose. Even he admitted it hurt. He also said I should take vitamin pills and get enough rest. How can I rest with all that homework to do? But I am determined not to have another nosebleed. I'm not having my nose smelted shut or whatever it is. Positive thinking will work. It will.

Did your mother really say "maybe" about coming out here next summer? A "maybe" is good. It isn't "no." It's something to work on.

Jack is coming by any minute. We're going to the Great Salt Lake to fly kites on the beach with Larry and Beth. He says everyone should get a close-up whiff of that lake at least once. I'm going to ask him to help me with my algebra.

What I miss about Holland is smoked eel, salted herring, and the potatoes. They brag about Idaho potatoes here, but they're nothing compared to Dutch potatoes. And, of course, I miss you. *Dag.*

> Kiss, kiss, kiss
> Annie

P.S. There's a boy in my English class—Woolley—who looks exactly like Edo. Really! He is the president of the high school (Don't you think it's odd to have a president of a high school?) Anyway, Henny loves him madly and has a date with him tonight.

Watching Henny get ready for her date with Woolley was sheer torture, still I couldn't miss it. Beth had asked me to go roller skating with her and Nedra, but I had made up an excuse. I wanted to see Tom Woolley come up our front walk, twice: once to pick Henny up and once to drop her off.

Henny tried on every article of clothing that she and I owned. None of it seemed good enough. She finally decided on gray wool slacks and a red bulky sweater. She took forever to put on her makeup, *sans* mole, but when she was done she looked really stunning.

I even told her so. I felt gloomy that she looked so stunning. They'll probably get married, and I'd covet my sister's husband for the rest of my life.

Woolley arrived in a white VW Beetle that looked spit-shined. He also wore a bulky sweater with some kind of design knitted into the front. I watched from the upstairs window, my breath wetting the glass.

"Oh my dear," I whispered. He and Henny looked too good together walking down the sidewalk to his car.

When they were gone, I watched the sky grow dark from my window and heaved sighs like a heroine in a gothic novel. I stood in front of the mirror and practiced puckering my lips. I unbuttoned several buttons of my shirt and pulled it off one shoulder and tried to look smoldering. I stuffed Kleenexes in my bra for a better bustline, but I just looked lopsided. I looked like a girl with Kleenexes stuffed into her bra. Finally I just lay on my bed in the dark.

I woke up when the overhead light blinked on. Henny stood over me. I lifted up on one elbow and rubbed my face.

"I'm in love," she said. "This is the real thing."

I sat up. I was disoriented and disappointed to have missed seeing Woolley for a second time that evening.

"What time is it?" I asked. My voice kind of croaked. "Where'd you go?"

"We went to Trolley Square—to the movies—and saw *Back to the Future.* He'd already seen it, but I hadn't. It's so funny!" She spun around and hugged herself. And after we went to that ice cream store across the street from the theater, you know, the one with the funny name . . ."

"Serendipity," I said.

"I'm in love. He was so cute, Henny. He told funny stories. He's really nice. And he's part Dutch. Can you believe it?"

"No kidding," I said. Listening to her was so depressing.

"He even knew how to say good-bye in Dutch. I taught him some other words." She snickered as she threw her shoes down.

"They're on my side of the room," I pointed out. I could picture Henny teaching Woolley Dutch. She got all animated and cute-looking when she got excited. I didn't want to think of her being attractive in any way.

She kicked her shoes under the bed. "He was so darling, Annie. Really, I had such a fantastic time!"

"Did he ask you out again?" I asked.

"No, but I know he had a good time too. You can just tell those things. So I think he will." She sighed, pulling her nightgown over her head. "He's just got to." The springs of her bed squeaked when she climbed in. "He's just got to," she repeated.

But the weeks went by, and Woolley didn't ask her out a second time. He joked with her in the halls at school, sat with her at lunch a couple of times (he and Jack had first lunch) and was an all-around super guy whenever he saw her, but he didn't ask her out. I was secretly glad, but I thought it a bit baffling too. I asked Maggie about it at lunch one day: "Why do you think Woolley hasn't asked Henny out again? She said they had a really great time together."

"Shh." she leaned into me and rolled her eyes toward Nedra, who was sitting at the end of the table. "Nedra thinks Woolley is her territory."

"Oh." I bent my head down. "Is he?"

"I don't know. Sort of. He takes Nedra out more than any other person, but he does date other girls sometimes. Frankly, I don't think Woolley wants to belong to anyone."

"Henny's frantic," I whispered.

"It's nothing personal. It's just Woolley's way—to float around and belong to everybody equally." She grimaced. "He's really kind of a big baby."

I disagreed but kept quiet.

Every day Henny quizzed me after school about Woolley. "What did he say to you today?"

"He asked me to marry him," I said one day. I sat at my desk in our bedroom.

"Oh sure," she groaned.

"He did," I said. "He's asked every girl in the class as far as I can tell."

"He hasn't asked me." Henny was practically suicidal. "What did you say?"

"I said yes." I meant it with all my heart even if he didn't, but I didn't tell her that.

"I'd marry him tomorrow," she said earnestly. I must have looked skeptical, because her voice grew louder. "I really would," she said.

I am just working up to kiss the back of his neck, I thought.

"Oh grow up!" I said it roughly.

"Grow up yourself. You don't have to be so pompous, just because you don't have any feelings yourself." She stomped out of the room.

I was glad she felt that way. It meant I hid my feelings well from her, from Jack, whom I didn't want to lose, and from Maggie. I didn't want Maggie to know how silly I was.

"Name your biggest secret," Maggie had commanded a few days before in the cafeteria. "A secret no one else knows."

I blushed as I opened the waxed paper for yet another

Vienna-sausage sandwich. Edo, Woolley: I was bogged down with secrets.

"Remember, I can read your mind," she said. She knitted her eyebrows into an expression that was supposed to be sinister.

I laughed. "I am secretly married to a tall, dark man from Istanbul. He hides under my bed, except at night he slides out and gets under the covers with me."

"Delicious." Maggie smacked her lips. "Then what?" she asked.

"Use your imagination," I said with a mouthful of bread and sausage.

"Like you do?" She opened little Tupperware bowls with various leftovers in them. Her lunch always seemed better than mine because of those Tupperware bowls. "Be serious now. I've got a wonderful secret that I've never told anyone. I'm bursting to tell it, but you have to tell me one first."

I yearn for Tom Woolley, I wanted to say. She would think I was crazy.

"Well," I said. "You know how Oma is always being blamed for stealing the Oreos and Twinkies—all the treats my mother buys?"

"Yes."

"And my mother has been hiding them in her sock drawer, and sometimes they still get stolen?"

"Yes."

"It isn't Oma," I said. "I steal them. I hoard them in my pillow case." I peeled a banana and stuffed the peel in my lunch sack.

Maggie was impressed. "That's evil," she said. "Does Henny know?"

"Of course not. In the first place, I don't want to share it with her. In the second place, she'd tell on me the first moment she got mad at me, which is every five minutes."

"You're very sneaky, Annie Sehlmeier," Maggie said.

"Thank you," I said. We grinned knowingly at each other.

"I've been dying to tell you mine." She giggled behind her cupped hands. "Remember when you met my father? How he was out to capture the newspaper thief?"

"I can hardly forget. He practically attacked me with a baseball bat."

"For two weeks he hadn't received his newspaper. It nearly drove him to drink. That's how he wakes up, you know. He reads it in bed, first thing in the morning." She paused, smiling down into a plastic bowl of canned peaches.

"I stole the newspapers myself!" she confessed, laughing a bit hysterically. "I did it. Me. *Moi!*"

"Why?" I really was surprised.

"Because I was so mad at him. Everytime I get upset about anything, he says, 'Relax, calm down. You can control yourself.' He can be so overbearing, so know-it-all. Like last year, when Mac and I had a fight, and we didn't go to the Christmas dance at all—I was really upset! 'That's life,' he said. 'You'll get over it.' He can be so smug. So I thought I'd show him a bit of life, myself." She spooned up some peaches. "And was he freaky. He practically blew up the house. And I said to him, 'Calm down,' I said. 'That's life,' I said." She laughed.

"You're such a sneak! I never would have thought of you doing that."

"It takes one to know one." She grinned.


In October Father bought a used car, a Buick station wagon, almost identical to Ome Gov's. He told Henny and me that we could learn to drive it. He said it would help Mother if we girls could drive her around and do errands for her. Mother didn't want to drive herself.

"We already know how to drive," Henny told him. I wasn't going to tell him myself. I was willing to pretend that I was learning for the first time.

"What do you mean?" he asked. We sat in the front of the Buick, inside the garage, where he had been pointing out what was what.

"Just what I said," Henny continued. "We already know how to drive. Farrah taught me, and Maggie and Jack taught Annie. She can even drive a truck!" Henny said proudly.

Father looked at me in amazement. "Is that true?" he asked.

I nodded my head.

"What if you'd had an accident? You'd have gone to jail without a license. What if . . ."

"We both have a learner's permit," Henny interrupted. Father still used an international driver's license he had acquired in Holland, because he was afraid his English wasn't good enough to take the written exam.

He gasped. "Have you two got any other secrets?"

I thought of telling him about the man from Istanbul hidden under my bed, but I decided he wouldn't like that joke.

"No sir," Henny said.

"Well then," he said feebly, opening the door, "I guess you don't need me to tell you where the ignition is located. You two had better go take your driver's test." He paused and shook his head.

"Thanks, Father," I called to him.

Henny's one date with Woolley had merely fanned the erotic flame in her tiresome bosom. She still burned to see him, and talk about him. She kissed his snapshots every evening before going to sleep. "He's the most perfect-looking human being in the world," she claimed again and again.

That's why she and Farrah always sat on the front row with me and Maggie at school assemblies: because Woolley sat with us. Maggie and I sat there, because we played the piano which was located just below the stage. Woolley sat there because, as president, he introduced and closed each assembly. Anyway, I had an excuse to sit in the front row with Tom

Woolley. Henny and Farrah were just making fools out of themselves. I told Henny a hundred times to stop acting like a jackass and that was *before* homecoming, which was the third assembly, when she really turned into a full-blown jackass—grew ears, practically.

Henny sat next to me on one side, Maggie on the other. Woolley's empty seat was next to her. Farrah sat on the aisle next to Henny. We all watched Woolley telling his stale jokes.

The audience laughed and shouted at the punch line. Henny blew a wolf whistle between her fingers.

I kicked her. "Don't do that," I said.

She said something obscene to me in Dutch.

Woolley welcomed the visitors and previewed the assembly briefly. When he finished, the spotlight moved from him to center stage, where the cheerleaders led by Nedra began a routine. Woolley descended the wooden steps left of the stage in the dark.

That was when Henny got up, ran to him, pulled him behind the upright piano, and kissed him on the mouth. I am talking passionate movie kissing here. Her arms were welded about his neck. He was stunned at first, but then put his arms around her shoulders and kissed her back.

It took about ten minutes.

It seemed like at least ten minutes.

Not very many kids saw it, because it was dark and they were off to one side, obscured partially by the piano, although there were a few catcalls from the left.

"Good grief," Maggie said. "She really has the hots for him."

"Wow," was all Farrah could muster. She was probably sorry she hadn't thought of it herself.

I felt heavy. My insides seemed filled with shifting marbles. It was humiliating having a sister like Henny. A sister with the "hots." A sister so out of control. I felt angry. I felt so ashamed. And I felt jealous.

The Tuesday after I got my driver's license, I drove Henny up to school for an evening Pep Club practice. On the way Henny came up with the idea of toilet-papering Woolley's car on consecutive Fridays for the rest of the school year.

"Are you completely nuts?" I said. Since the homecoming assembly I was convinced she needed to be institutionalized. "Where did you get such an idea?"

"From Farrah. She says kids do it all the time. Sometimes they toilet-paper a whole house. Anyway, we could do it every single Friday. We must never skip a week. Pretty soon he'll begin to expect it." Her eyes widened. "It'll become dangerous. We could get caught. He'd be waiting, wondering when we were coming. And as cunning as we'd be, we'd always be wondering if he was hiding somewhere, ready to jump out at us." She squealed at the very thought, brought her legs up to her chest and hugged them. "The suspense would be delicious."

"What do you mean, *we*?" I asked her. There was a parking space in front of the gymnasium. I pulled in. A couple of girls with red and white pompoms walked past the front of the car.

Henny laughed. "You'd have to go with me. I couldn't do it alone." She grabbed my arm.

"Take Farrah then. It's her idea."

"Farrah's too stupid. She'd get caught the first day. Besides she talks too much."

I was surprised by this statement.

"No way," I said, pulling away from her. "Why would you want to do such a dumb thing?" I already knew the answer before she spoke it.

Her eyes searched the football field. "Because," she murmured. "It's a way of being involved with him no matter how indirect. It's a way of feeling close to him."

I sighed. "It's stupid," I said. "It's childish."

"Thanks a lot." She climbed out of the car and slammed the door shut.

I backed the car out. Henny walked hurriedly to the side door of the gym without looking at me. I could tell from her gait she was angry. Instead of driving down 8th South toward home, I drove up to Emigration Canyon. I thought about her idea of covering Woolley's car with toilet paper every Friday night, in the dark, close to his house. Close to him. Perhaps we would catch a glimpse of him through a window, eating or talking with his parents. My heart beat faster.

The sky was cloudless. I lowered the window and let the wind blow my hair.

If I did it, if I went with her, I would be like her. I would be like a person who kissed her high school president in back of the piano at assembly.

No, I wasn't anything like that. I really loved Woolley. It made me sick, I loved him so much. Real love. It was different with Henny. She had the hots. That was different from love. I was in love.

I liked Jack too. We flew kites again in the dark on the playing field across the street from my house. We ate sundaes at the Garden Gate. He told me he was applying to Stanford as well as the University of Utah for next year. If Stanford gave him a scholarship, he'd go there. He couldn't afford it without one. We kissed on the front porch until Father blinked the yellow porch light on and off, and I had to go in. I liked kissing Jack. I liked Jack too.

I wondered where Woolley lived. I thought about getting caught toilet-papering his car. It made my palms sweaty just to think of it.

When I picked Henny up, I was prepared to tell her that I would go with her.

She got in the car and said, "I'll pay you five dollars a week if you will just drive me to Woolley's house or wherever, and I'll do the toilet-papering. You won't even have to get out of the car." She stuffed the pompoms behind her legs.

"Okay," I said. I couldn't believe how well this was all going. "But," I continued, "don't tell a soul. Absolutely no one. That includes Farrah, and I will only drive. I will be the —what do they call them in the movies?"

"The getaway man."

"Yes. I will be the getaway man, but you can't tell anyone. Promise?"

"Promise!" She squeezed my arm. She was so grateful.

"Woolley's definitely not worth it," I lied, wondering if I was getting demerits in heaven. "I think the whole scheme is the dumbest thing I ever heard of. It's insane."

"Yeah, yeah. Don't get hyper."

I pulled up to the front of the house. Oma sat on Mr. Eberley's front steps.

"Oh gosh, what is she doing?" I said.

"Waiting for her true love to come out of the house, I imagine." Henny shook her head. "It's so hopeless." She walked to the house.

I went down to fetch Oma. "Let's go home and eat dinner," I said to her.

"Not until Jacob comes out of the house." She folded her arms tightly, as if she intended to stay forever.

"He's not Jacob," I said. "He's Mr. Eberley."

She glared at me without answering.

The front door opened, startling me. Mr. Eberley stepped onto the porch. Oma stood up, her face radiant at the sight of him. "Jacob," she whispered. She reached up to stroke his cheek.

Mr. Eberley stepped back stiffly.

"I'm sorry," I said quickly in English. "My grandmother's senile, and she still thinks that you're her husband. She calls

112

you Jacob," I said. "Come on Oma," I said in Dutch and pulled her arm.

"Nay," she said nastily and shoved me away. "Jacob," she said again.

Mr. Eberley stared down at Oma. "What's her name?" he asked me.

"Johanna," I said, giving it the Dutch pronunciation.

"Johanna," he said to Oma putting her arm through his and leading her down the steps. Oma smiled at him. She wore a skirt and blouse covered with an apron. Soft wisps of hair floated out of the bun on her head.

Mr. Eberley led her up the street to our house and then passed it.

"We live here," I called.

"We'll walk around the block once and then home," he said.

"She doesn't speak any English," I reminded him.

"I can call her by her name. That will be enough," he said. They disappeared around the corner.

On Friday night Henny and I just about died when Mother and Father said they were going to a wedding reception in Provo, an hour away, and we wouldn't be able to use the car.

"We need it," Henny demanded.

Father informed her that the tail did not wag the dog in this family.

"Can we take the truck?" Henny asked anxiously. "I have to go see *Amadeus,* this movie about Mozart. I have to write a report on it for Monday. It's downtown," she said.

"You can go tomorrow," Mother said.

"No, I can't. I have to go tonight. There's going to be a lecture after the movie. Some professor from the university is giving it. I have to be there." Henny was a terrific liar. I admired her quickness.

"Maybe you can go with Farrah," Mother suggested. "You

113

can't both go, in any case, because somebody has to stay with Oma."

Henny groaned out loud. I groaned inwardly. Oma again. Always Oma.

While Henny and I were still washing dishes, Mother and Father left for Provo. Mother had helped Oma into her nightgown so Henny and I wouldn't have to do it. Oma sat at the kitchen table watching us. "You don't do the dishes as well as your mother," she observed icily.

"Thanks," Henny said.

I was disappointed about postponing our plan to decorate Woolley's car. I had secretly looked up his address. He lived in the same neighborhood as Maggie, on Macalester Street.

"We can start next week," I said to Henny, who was practically throwing dishes into the drainer.

"No, we'll go tonight. It's always going to be complicated," she said. "You can drive the truck."

"It has SEHLMEIER printed all over it," I said.

"So what? We'll park it a block away."

"What about Oma? We can't leave her alone," I reminded her.

"We'll take her with us." She dumped the dirty dish water into the sink.

"We can't!" I protested. "She could yell or do something crazy."

"No, she won't." She opened the refrigerator door and pulled out a package of Twinkies. "You can feed her these while I do the toilet-papering." She grinned at me. "Good idea, no?"

"No."

The drive in the truck to Woolley's house only took about five minutes. Henny knew exactly where it was. I only killed the engine a couple of times, usually at stop lights. I wasn't real good with the clutch yet. Woolley's white VW was parked in front of his house under a street light.

"It's too dangerous with that light right there," I whispered to Henny as we cruised past the car.

"I'll work fast," said Henny. "Do you see him?" She was looking up at the house. I lowered my head. The windows of his house were all lit up, but I didn't see any people and said so.

"Let me out here," Henny said at the corner, a roll of toilet paper in her grasp. "Go around the block and stop about a half block from the house." She unraveled the toilet paper.

I parked far enough away to feel somewhat safe, but at a distance near enough to watch Henny and Woolley's house. I crouched down behind the steering wheel.

"What are you doing?" Oma asked in Dutch. To anyone looking in, she was sitting alone in the cab of the truck.

"I'm hiding from Henny," I said. I pulled a Twinkie out of my coat pocket. "Would you like this?" She grabbed at it. "Eat it slowly," I said.

I was crunched down for several minutes and had to go to the bathroom something awful. One leg was asleep. After a while I poked my head up to see how Henny was doing. The car was already covered. Henny was tying long pieces of toilet paper to the antenna.

Then I saw him. Even from a distance, I knew it was him. He was standing at a side window at what seemed to be the kitchen sink. My mouth grew dry. If he turned his head, he would be able to see Henny. I wanted to honk, but that would get Woolley's attention too. It's finished, Henny, I thought. Come back now. Henny began wrapping the windshield wipers carefully. I dug in my pocket for the other Twinkie, my palms sticky. "Here, Oma," I said. I handed it to her. "Eat this and stay here," I commanded. "Stay!"

I opened the door softly and moved around the back of the

truck and onto the sidewalk. I ran on tiptoes to a cluster of fir trees on the lawn next door to Woolley's house.

"Pssst," I called from the trees.

Henny looked down the street at the truck. Oma sat in it alone, eating a Twinkie.

"Here," I whispered as loud as I dared. "Come here. Over here in the trees." Her eyes searched in the direction of my voice. I stepped out briefly and frantically waved my arms. She rolled the remaining toilet paper under the car and ran over to me.

"He's standing right by the window. If he turned his head, he'd see you for sure," I whispered. I had to go to the bathroom so badly. Henny stepped out of the trees and hid behind the bushes that separated Woolley's yard from the one we were in.

"Oh my gosh," she said, and squealed.

"Let's go," I whispered. My bladder was bursting.

Henny led out to the sidewalk and then pushed me back into the trees. "There's a car coming." She motioned down to the truck. We waited for a moment, and then both of us leaned cautiously out of the trees. The car, its headlights shining in our direction, had stopped adjacent to Father's truck.

"Is it the police?" I whispered. Henny had her neck craned further than mine.

She pulled back. "Worse," she whispered. "It's Maggie and her parents."

I immediately wet my pants. "Oh jeez," I breathed.

"Shhh." She waved her hand at me.

I heard Maggie's voice. "She's all alone in here," she was saying to her parents.

"Mr. Sehlmeier must be close by," Dr. Connors said.

"She's not supposed to be alone," Maggie said. "She walks away sometimes."

"It's odd they left her in the truck by herself—in her night-gown, even." This was Mrs. Connors's voice.

"Daddy, let's go home and call the Sehlmeiers. It will only take a minute." She got back into the car.

"The girls are hiding in the trees!" Oma shouted suddenly. "They're in the trees!" She pointed in our direction. Henny and I crouched into what we hoped was an invisible heap. Then I realized that they couldn't understand Oma's Dutch. She was speaking Dutch. My heart was beating like a budgie in a box.

The Connors' car made a U-turn back in the direction of Maggie's house.

"Let's go," ordered Henny. We scampered to the truck. It took three tries to start the engine. The seat of my pants was cold with urine.

"Go, go, go!" commanded Henny, nervously.

I let my foot off the clutch as carefully as I could, but the truck leaped and bumped forward like a bucking bronco.

"I'm going to tell your mother on you, about hiding in the bushes," Oma said as we were safely cruising down 8th South.

Henny and I burst into a loud, nervous guffaw.

"I am," said Oma. "You girls are nothing but hoodlums."

We both knew that by morning she would have forgotten all about it.

Maggie did mention seeing Oma. She said that she had tried to call our house without success, and when she and her parents got back to where Oma had been, she and the truck were gone. I told her I didn't know anything about it, that Henny and I had gone to see *Amadeus* downtown. It was the first time I had lied to Maggie, who was my very best friend in America, but this was something she must never know.

At school, Woolley's handsome neck tantalized me more than ever.

The second Friday night was a high school football game. Henny excused herself from our group in the bleachers, said she had to go to the bathroom, and toilet-papered Woolley's car in the school parking lot. She said it took her twenty minutes just to find it. I was glad I didn't have to go with her.

The third week we had to wait over an hour for Woolley to come home from wherever he was, and when he was safely in the house, Henny toilet-papered the VW in record time while I waited, crouched down in the Buick. When Henny got in the car, she whispered, "Look up to the second floor." We were in the back of the house, in the alley. Woolley's car was parked in front of the garage.

I looked up. Woolley was removing his shirt. I let out an involuntary gasp. I had seen the black hair on his chest and, oh awesome, I had seen his navel. My insides shuffled about. I felt dizzy. He was so beautiful.

Henny fanned herself with an empty envelope. "He's so beautiful," she swooned.

"Don't be an idiot," I snapped. "Haven't you ever seen a boy's chest before?"

"Wake up, Annie, that is not a *boy's* chest."

"This is so stupid," I said, starting up the car. I didn't turn the lights on. "I don't know why I do this."

"For the money, sister dear. For the money." She placed the five dollars on the dashboard.

I will go to Hell, I thought. I felt weak all over.

By the fourth Friday we figured Woolley would be expecting us, maybe even watching for us, so we went early in the morning. It went without a hitch. I was so relaxed I fell asleep.

On the fifth Friday Henny skipped first period and toilet-papered Woolley's car in broad daylight in the school parking lot.

On the sixth week I almost became an only child. Henny had decided it was safe enough to go back to Woolley's house in the evening. I drove her up at about 9:00 P.M. The white

VW was parked again in front of the garage in back of Woolley's house. For a few minutes, I watched Henny work, the Buick idling in the alley, but then noticing that the driveway across the alley from Woolley's was vacant, I backed the Buick into that and shut off the engine. Crouching down in the front seat, I watched Henny. She had begun to make a ritual of the toilet-papering, unraveling long streamers, waving them above her head while she danced, finally allowing them to fall on the car. She tied streamers to the back and front bumpers and laid them out on the cement driveway. She made a fluffy sort of pompom to stick on the end of the antenna.

I watched this rather dreamily through the steering wheel when the back door of Woolley's house opened. A stream of light broke loose from the interior. Henny, hearing the door, bent down behind the car.

"I'll only be about an hour," Woolley's voice called. My heart pumped anxiously. Henny looked over her shoulder at me, probably trying to decide if she could run for it, but the alley was illuminated by a bright arc light, and Woolley would have seen her for sure. Instead, she dragged herself directly under his car, lying flat on her stomach.

"Oh Lord," I whispered.

"Dammit," Woolley blasted. "Not again." He tore away the toilet paper that had just been lovingly placed there by my sister and dumped it into a nearby trash can. Then he got into the driver's seat of the car.

I was crouched down as far as I could be and still see him. "Get out from under the car, Henny," I thought. "Please get out."

Woolley started the engine and revved it a couple of times. Henny lay motionless.

I sat straight up. I should get out and stop him, I thought, but I was frozen into position. I recalled a cat I had once seen

119

mashed on the asphalt parking lot of a church. I wanted to throw up.

Woolley backed up, turning as he reached the alley. I watched through the fingers of my hands. "Oh Lord," I breathed again. He shifted the car and drove impatiently forward, the tires spitting gravel as he disappeared.

Henny lay there.

I got out of the car and ran to her. "Henny," I said.

"Has he gone?" she asked rolling over stiffly.

"Are you all right?" I pulled on her arm. She sat up.

"Yeah." She brushed off the front of her coat. "I thought I was dead for a minute." She looked up at me and began to snicker helplessly. "Can you believe it?" She laughed behind cupped hands. "Can you absolutely believe it? I could have touched his foot," she gasped.

"Let's get out of here," I said.

She stood up, laughing and snorting the whole time.

"Shh," I hushed. "Someone might hear us. It could be embarrassing." We both climbed into the car. Henny collapsed into the front seat and broke into unrestrained laughter.

"You're insane," I said, glad to be driving out of that alley. "This is the last time I'm going to do this." I still felt nauseous.

Henny stopped giggling. "Don't be such a poop," she said. "You weren't in any danger."

"No," I said. "I just get left behind to explain to Father and Mother how you happened to get run over in someone's driveway."

She shrieked. I loosened into a smile.

"You'll go again, won't you?"

"I'll see."

"That means yes. At least you know you're alive," she said. "I'm not boring."

"No, you're definitely not boring, Henny."

I did go again, of course, right through the fall, a couple of times long after our parents had gone to bed.

At school Woolley reported on Monday morning to those of us who sat around him about the toilet paper hit-man.

"More likely hit-woman," Jack mused.

"An admirer," I said.

"He doesn't have any admirers," Beth said, sticking her tongue out at him.

"Is it you, Marvelous Meryl?" Woolley breathed his fragrant breath on me.

"Yes, it is," I said, looking straight into his handsome face. Jack guffawed. "I help her," he said.

Woolley snarled: "Don't do it again just before it rains. It took me an hour and a half to clean up the mess."

Beth and I said at the same time: "Poor baby."

He was still complaining about it when we entered choir. Maggie, who met us in the hall, said, "Why don't we wait up for the culprit? We could sit in your garage. It has a window in it, doesn't it?"

Woolley thought this was a great idea. "This Friday," he said. The irony almost choked me to death. I could barely wait to tell Henny.

On Friday night, a whole crowd of us, Jack and me, Beth and Larry, Maggie and Roger, Woolley and Nedra, Farrah and Flash sat in Woolley's cold and damp garage, eating M&M's and Fritos until one o'clock in the morning.

"I've got to go home." I nudged Jack, who had fallen asleep on my shoulder. Everyone agreed it was time to leave. We shuffled sleepily about while Woolley opened the garage door. "Maybe we scared her away for one night anyway," he said.

When I got back I turned off the light above the stove that Mother left on when she knew I was going to be home late and tiptoed upstairs.

"Henny," I shook her. "It's time to go," I said.

That night, Henny created her *magnum opus*. Using the VW as the center of the design, she made spokes of toilet paper and connected them to low tree branches and bushes, so that the entire yard looked like a fluttering spider's web.

Jack and I went to the Christmas dance and laughed and sang in each other's ear. He looked like an ad in *The New Yorker* in his navy blue suit, and I looked as good as Meryl Streep in my black velvet dress with the white lace collar. During the intermission we stood arm in arm watching the crowning of the Snow King and Queen: Woolley and Nedra Stone. Her hair was black as Woolley's and she wore a white diaphanous gown that was probably purchased in heaven.

Nedra was presented with a bouquet of roses and a large gold box of chocolates. She and Woolley were both crowned with gold sparkly crowns that glittered in the light when they turned their heads. Woolley reached over and kissed Nedra, and everyone clapped and cheered. Jack wore an amused, slightly cynical look on his face, but he applauded too.

After the ceremonies, Woolley and Nedra stopped by the table where Jack and I sat drinking punch.

"Have a piece of my candy," Nedra offered. "They're practically sinful, they're so good." She pushed the open box across the table. The chocolates were individually wrapped in gold tinsel. Jack and I each took one. Nedra and Woolley took one too. The chocolate was extraordinarily rich.

"What are these?" I cried. "They're out of this world."

"Food for Snow Kings and Queens," Jack said, his mouth full of chocolate. He squeezed my hand.

"They're truffles," said Nedra. "Aren't they scrumptious?" She gave us the full, practiced, glamour smile, all the perfect pearlies showing, only one front tooth was completely blacked out with chocolate.

I glanced at Jack whose eyes gleamed devilishly. "They're good all right." He smiled. I kicked his foot under the table.

"They're a cure for cancer," I said.

Jack snorted.

"You look more like Meryl Streep than ever tonight." Woolley wooed me from across the table. "Will you dance one with me?"

Jack released my hand under the table. I followed Woolley out to the dance floor. Jack and Nedra followed us. Woolley held me so tightly, I was afraid my legs wouldn't move, not that I wanted him to loosen his grip any. I didn't. My nose was practically in his neck, exactly where I had wanted it to be all fall in Mr. Crow's English class. His aftershave, that magical aphrodisiac, floated into my nostrils, and as I was about to close my eyes and fall into a swoon more or less, I saw Jack making faces at me over Nedra's shoulder and burst into wild giggling. Woolley stopped dancing. "I thought I was a good dancer," he said.

"It's Jack." I pointed but Jack had disappeared into the crowd.

We began dancing again. "You really like Jack, don't you?" Woolley said.

"I really do," I said. "He makes me laugh." I thought of all the times I had been with Jack when I was thinking of Woolley, and now here I was dancing with Woolley and thinking of Jack. It felt good.

After the dance Jack and I stood under the yellow light of the porch and held each other, our faces touching.

"I feel like I'm hugging a bear." Jack laughed, his mouth was close to my ear, his face was warm and smelled of spice. I was wearing a fat winter coat.

"You smell wonderful," I couldn't help saying.

"You are wonderful. I like you better than . . ."

"Life itself," I finished for him.

"No, that's no good." He laughed. "Sounds like Woolley, the golden throat of insincerity."

I drew my head back so I could see his face. "You think that?" I asked. "But he's your friend."

"He wouldn't be if he talked to me the way he talks to girls. I'd want to throw up. Like the way he's always telling you that you look like Meryl Streep. It's so insulting."

"But Meryl Streep is lovely," I argued. "It's flattering to be compared with her."

"Yes, but you're you. You're not one of those made-up movie star fantasies. You're real. You're better. I think you're prettier, for that matter." He said this almost without thinking and then blushed.

"I heard that," I said.

We kissed.

"You like me better than what? I'm still waiting for a dazzling metaphor to knock me off my feet." I hugged his neck. I was having a good time.

"I like you better than," he reached into his overcoat pocket, "chocolate truffles." He held up a single truffle wrapped in gold.

"Another one? Where'd you get it?" My mouth watered instantly.

"I stole it out of the Snow Queen's box." He unwrapped it carefully. "You get first bite, remembering that I get what's left." He held it just out of reach.

"Promise not to snarf it!" he said.

"I promise." I bit into half the truffle, which had a creamy dark chocolate center. We kissed with the chocolate still in our mouths.

The porch light blinked on and off impatiently. Jack and I separated, both of us acutely aware of my father's glaring presence on the other side of the glass door.

"I had a very pleasant evening," Jack said in a loud voice, shaking my hand.

"The pleasure was all mine. Thank you."

We both laughed. I watched as he stepped off the porch and ran to his car, his breath visible in the cold night. He called back from his car in an exaggerated whisper: "I like you more than chocolate truffles, Annie Sehlmeier!"

"I like you too," I called back.

That night I went to bed and dreamed only of Jack Wakefield.


I bought Henny a bracelet of cultured pearls connected with a gold chain for Christmas. She had shown me one like it in a magazine. I could afford it because of the extra money I got for driving her to Woolley's house every Friday night. Besides that, buying it for her mollified my conscience somewhat for taking the money in the first place. I wrapped it, sitting on the floor of my bedroom while Henny was at Farrah's. I placed the box with the bracelet in it inside a roll of toilet paper and began wrapping it in red tissue.

"What are you doing?" Oma stood in the doorway, hands in her apron pocket.

I started a little. I hadn't heard her come up the stairs. "I'm wrapping a present for Henny," I said. I curled the ribbon with the scissors.

She sat on the bed carefully and began to sing in a soft low voice a lullaby that she used to sing to me when I was very young. She would sit on the floor with me in her lap. We would clap our hands together and place them on our heads and make waves for the ship as the song indicated. I turned to look at her.

She nodded. "Do you remember when we used to sing that?" She motioned her hands, fingers outspread, into waves and repeated the last line—the line about the ships.

"Yes," I said. I was amazed that she remembered it.

"Then I made you chocolate pudding poured into little sculptured molds because you liked the shapes so much." She

125

covered her mouth with one hand and laughed. "And you would get so mad if the molded pudding fell apart, because you wanted it perfect!" She smiled.

"It hardly ever fell apart. You always did it perfectly," I said. "You did everything perfectly."

"Not everything." She sighed. She gazed out the window. "I wish I could go back," she said. She began humming very softly, her head bobbing with the tune. I hugged her about the waist and lay my head in her lap. "Oma, I wish you could stay like this all the time."

She stroked my head and continued humming. She stopped abruptly. Her hand on my hair. "I am such a bother now," she said.

I closed my eyes. "We don't mind. None of us minds. You're not a bother," I assured her, but as much as I wanted that to be true, I knew our relationship, like her memory of the past, was as fragile as the glass angel on our Christmas tree.

Kaatje Tefsen
Domstraat 18
Utrecht, The Netherlands
New Year's Day

Dear Kaatje,

Thank you, thank you for the wonderful necklace. I haven't taken it off since Christmas morning. I had a wonderful Christmas which I will tell you about, but it was punctuated with a kind of sadness that I couldn't quite shake off: Oma took a turn for the worse. She didn't come out of her room at all on Christmas Day, but just sat quietly on her bed staring into space.

I got the most wonderful pair of expensive red shoes for Christmas. Mother went with me when I tried them on, but she clucked her tongue at the price and said I'd have to be happy with something a little less extravagant, and then she went right back and bought them. They're exquisite.

Jack and I exchanged cultural stockings for Christmas, so to speak. He gave me a stocking his mother had made filled with trinkets and candies, including a small box of truffles and a used book on algebra written in Chinese—I don't know where he found it. He wrote a note asking me if the Chinese directions were more explicit. He's been explaining the English algebra directions to me all term and has literally saved my hide. I'm getting a B+ in there, which is a lot better than failing. I gave him a pair of wooden shoes his size (there are two Dutch import stores in Salt Lake) filled with straw and small presents including a small Dutch-English dictionary, a chocolate letter J, and a jar of pickled herring, which he said was the most putrid present he'd ever received. He walked over in the evening, and we began a game of Scrabble which was never finished, because Roger Thompson came down to give Henny a pocket version of Trivial Pursuit. Maggie fixed her up with him for the Christmas dance, and they really hit it off. Anyway, we ended up calling Maggie and Larry and Beth and even Farrah and Flash and had a long and loud game that didn't break up until after midnight when Father came out in his bathrobe to announce that it was late. Henny walked Roger out to the Reverend Moon, where I noticed they hugged good-bye. Maybe Roger will get her mind off Woolley, although his pictures still adorn the wall above her bed. After Henny went upstairs, Jack and I did a lot of Christmas kissing in the vestibule without interruption from my father, who had finally given up the ghost and gone to sleep. A flourish of Christmas trumpets!

That was a week ago. Now it's afternoon and Ome

Govert is explaining football to my father as they watch it on the television. Mother and Geert are sitting with Oma in her bedroom. She still refuses to come out. Henny has gone to bed, because she doesn't feel good. At first she thought she was tired, because she and Roger went to a church dance last night but she feels even worse this afternoon.

I've had only one little teeny-weeny nosebleed since visiting the doctor and that was at school so my mother didn't know. I told you positive thinking would work. I've cured myself.

Write me after Edo's wedding and tell me all about it. Send pictures! Give your mother my love. Happy New Year! Mine is going to be terrific.

> Kiss, kiss, kiss
> Annie

It didn't hurt at all to think about Edo's wedding coming up in a month. I was finished with all that. I was finished with Woolley too. I had decided that on Christmas night, kissing Jack in the vestibule of my house. Jack was my only true love.

I thought Henny might be finished with Woolley too now that Roger was on the scene but she still insisted on toilet-papering his car the Friday nights during the holidays. She said it wouldn't be a good joke unless it was done for the whole school year. The Friday before Christmas we arrived at Woolley's house in time to follow him to the Cottonwood Mall to go shopping. We toilet-papered the VW there in the parking lot, and Henny left a small tin of fudge on the hood of the car (Juffrouw deWaart calls the hood of a car the "bonnet," but I learned quickly not to call it that in America).

Henny got the flu and wasn't able to return to school. Her temperature rose to 104 degrees, and Dr. Wirthlin said that she might have to go to the hospital. Mother spent one whole night with her, pressing cold packs on her forehead, feeding her aspirin. I slept on the sofa in the living room, or rather lay awake, watching the strange shadows form in the changing light from the outside. I knew Henny would not be able to toilet-paper Woolley's car that Friday, so the ritual would be broken. Certainly, I wasn't going to risk it.

On Thursday, I took the bus to the downtown library after school to work on a term paper I was writing for Mr. Crow's class. It was a research paper on *Macbeth,* which we had read before Christmas. I climbed the stairs to the second floor of the library where the research room was located. I laid my books on a table in the corner by the windows and walked across the room to the periodical guide and made notations in my notebook. Then I checked out several journals. On the way back to my table, the heavy wooden door opened and Woolley walked in with an armload of books. He grinned when he saw me. "Where are you sitting?" he asked in a whisper. His cheeks were red from the cold. He had no pores that I could see. I pointed to the corner.

"I'll be over in a second," he said. He laid several books on the librarian's desk and had a brief, whispered conversation with her. She blushed when she spoke to him. She'd probably write his paper for him, if he asked her, I thought.

I began marking certain paragraphs from one article.

He sat down next to me, his coat thrown over the back of the chair. He wore a new sweater, of dark green with two red reindeer facing each other on the front. His face was tanned from skiing over the holidays. He looked absolutely stunning, and I felt my Christmas-day resolve fading. The pure physical beauty of him made me weak and dizzy.

"How are you doing?" He leaned into me and smiled.

I didn't move away. I smiled back without answering.

He opened a book and pretended to read the same way I pretended to read. His body seemed to give off electrical charges. My insides trembled like Oma's chocolate pudding. I tried following the text with my pencil, marking lightly each sentence as I read it. For a half hour, I worked in that tremulous state.

Then Woolley reached over and wrote lightly in my notebook, "I love Annie Sehlmeier." He watched my face while I read it. I swallowed. I did not believe it, but I liked seeing it written in his hand. My face burned.

I wrote in his notebook, "You love all the girls!" I felt his breath on my cheek while I wrote. He smacked his lips and glanced briefly at the librarian. He's teasing us both, I thought.

"Only the fairest in the land," he wrote.

"CUT IT OUT," I printed in heavy block letters.

"Don't you like me?" he whispered, his face in that well practiced pout.

"You're adorable," I said, "but you're never serious."

"Does that matter so very much?"

An irrational inner voice barked at me: "Go make out with him in the stacks. Now's your chance."

A more rational voice called Jack's name to me.

"I'll learn to be serious for you," Woolley said, crossing his heart. His lips were almost on mine.

I laughed too loudly. The librarian looked up. I covered my mouth. "You're pathological," I said.

"Do you like it?" His mouth brushed my cheek.

"You have a certain charm," I laughed, and stood up. "I'm going home," I said. "I'm not going to get anything done sitting next to you."

"How about a kiss before you go?"

I blew him one.

"I prefer you in the flesh," he said, grinning.

I walked out into the street where a light snow was falling. I prefer you in the flesh too, and it's too scary to think about.

130

When I arrived home, Mother and Father were putting on their coats. "Oma has disappeared," Father said quickly. "We're going out to look for her. Bishop Wakefield has gathered some neighbors who are also out looking. Geert is upstairs with Henny." He pulled his gloves on.

"There's fried potatoes and Polish sausage in the pot." Mother nodded toward the stove.

"What about the police?" I asked.

"They've been notified. We have to go." Father waved me off impatiently.

"She's not even wearing a coat," Mother said in a stricken voice as they went out the back door.

I stood alone in the kitchen. The phone rang. "I'll get it," I called upstairs. It was Jack.

"I just got home and heard about Oma," he said.

"I just heard about it myself," I said. "Mother and Father just left to go look for her."

"I don't know if it'll help, but I thought I'd go look too. Do you want to come?"

I told him I did.

"I'll pick you up in fifteen minutes," he said and hung up.

I ate my dinner quickly and changed into warmer clothing upstairs.

"How cold is it?" Henny asked. An empty dinner plate rested on her night table.

"About twenty-five degrees," I muttered, fastening my belt buckle.

"Maybe, she'll be okay," mused Tante Geert, but I knew she didn't believe it.

Jack and I walked in the snow through backyards, searching in play houses and Mr. Eberley's vacant garage. "We should really go look on his front porch," I said to Jack. "That's where she liked to sit the most." Jack shone his flashlight into every shadowy corner of the large wraparound porch and then did it again.

"She's not here now," he muttered.

We walked to the church around the corner, where Oma had wandered several times, and searched the dark entryways, the clustered shrubbery, the parking lot. We searched the junior high school in the same way.

The snow fell wet and heavy. We walked to Liberty Park to the concession area, where Oma had gone once, but there were so many places to hide, it was hopeless.

We went home. I gave Jack a hug by my back door. "Thanks," I said. "If they don't find her, I don't think I'll be at school tomorrow."

He nodded. "We were going to Maggie's party tomorrow night," he reminded me. "Do you still want to go?"

"I don't know," I said. "Mother might need me."

"I'll call you," he said.

I kissed him lightly. "Good night," I said. "And thanks again." I went into the house.

I didn't go to school on Friday, nor did I go to Maggie's party with Jack, but sat with Henny in the bedroom, watching out the window at the stream of people who came by to check with my parents, some of them policemen. Father and Mother came and went, searching the same places again and again. Oma was not to be found.

It was warmer than it had been the day before. The snow was melted from the sidewalks and streets. Henny dozed a lot, leaving me to my own thoughts. I gazed at the picture of Jack and me that my father had taken before the Christmas dance, which was now taped above my bed. And then I looked at the two pictures of Woolley above Henny's bed. If I loved anyone, it would be Jack, but why could Woolley merely breathe on me and turn me into a blithering idiot? I opened my notebook and read Woolley's handwriting. "I love Annie Sehlmeier."

Henny awoke once and asked me meekly if I wouldn't please go toilet-paper Woolley's car that night. "We were going to do it for the whole school year. Now it will be spoiled," she sighed.

"Forget it," I said. "I won't do it. It's too risky. Besides, it's inappropriate when Oma's missing this way. I wouldn't go even if you were well."

She turned her face to the wall with the photos on it, and sighed.

Late that night Oma still had not been found. I lay in bed, awake, feeling the pull of Tom Woolley.

I love Annie Sehlmeier.

I love Annie Sehlmeier.

I love Annie Sehlmeier.

# PART 5

## *Humiliations*

I listened to Henny's breathing. Often she turned noisily in the bed, and once she almost sat up and said something I couldn't hear. I waited. The light from the street made odd shadows on the ceiling. Occasionally a car passed by, and once a train whistle blew in the far distance. Where are the people going at three in the morning? Why aren't they in their beds? Oma, perhaps, was out there. Who are the night people?

Even as I thought this, I was getting out of bed and feeling my way into my jeans. I put them on over my flannel pajamas. I put on my socks and my parka and carried my boots to the front door away from my parents, who slept in the back of the house. The front door was safe. I put on my boots in the front vestibule and bumped into a small table with my behind when I bent to tug the boot.

Silence, except for the night sounds: the hum of the refrigerator, the clock on the dining-room wall. I tied the boots, opened the front door and was out on the porch. I was dressed too warmly—it felt almost like spring, mild—mild enough for Oma to sleep outside for two nights? I shuddered. Mustn't think of Oma. Only of Woolley. What a triumph to paper the car on this night. Alone. Without Henny. Alone. A ritual of love. I would do something wonderful with the car. It would be my masterpiece. Mine.

When I opened the car door, the interior light glared in the darkness. Hurriedly I pulled the door shut. The light blinked off. The toilet paper was in the backseat where I had stashed it earlier. Nervously I inserted the key into the ignition and turned it. It began immediately. I held my breath and watched the black windows at the back of our house. I expected to see their light on, my parents' faces peering at me through the glass.

Off with her head!

I backed the car out of the alley. No light on anywhere. The Spivacks, the Keddingtons, Miss Rifkin were all sleeping, never knowing that I had become a night person. It was different than when I went with Henny. That was a prank. I had gone through a change. I was obsessed, and obsessions are serious business. I read it in the *Ladies' Home Journal.*

Woolley's block was lit by two street lights, one at either end. I drove slowly past his house and hummed a generic tune. His car was not in the street, so it had to be in the alley. I blew a kiss up to the house before turning the corner. A part of me, a rather distant part, I admit, warned me against myself. "You're acting like a fool." It was really quite faint.

I blew another kiss. "Hello, my love, I'm here," I said aloud. I felt so brave. Really, this was going to be fun. I didn't need Henny to show me how to live my life. I could do it alone.

Woolley's white VW was parked directly in front of the garage door. I turned off the car lights and stopped in the middle of the alley adjacent to his car. The car glowed in the moonlight. Clutching the toilet paper, I got out of the passenger side of my car and shut the door. The click of the latch thundered over the neighborhood. I leaned against the door and waited again for lights to flash on.

Woolley's car was shining. I unwrapped the toilet paper and thought for several minutes. Wrapping the car wasn't enough. It was the same old thing that Henny did. What could I do differently? I ran my hand across the cool metal front of the car and then onto the bumper, and sideways across the doors, outlining each window with an index finger. I felt the back of the car, the part that covered the engine.

It was warm!

I stood still and listened.

How warm was it? I tried to think. Not that warm. How long does it take for an engine to cool? How long?

I turned all the way around and willed my eyes to see through the darkness. I didn't see anyone. I stood perfectly still, aware of the blood pumping through my veins. Aware. I stood like that for hours. It seemed like hours.

Then I unraveled the toilet paper and wrapped some around my body, over the down jacket, around my neck, around my head and let the streamers fall down my back and across my arms and I began to dance to a tuneless rhythm. I danced around the car, and stroked it with my palms and swayed over it and swirled around again and again to an imaginary string orchestra. I put my arms up as if I were dancing with him—Woolley—and I waltzed on the cement, on the toes of my boots, the very tiptoes of my boots. I will dance the ritual dance. I will be the virgin sacrifice.

A receding inner voice barked, "Nonsense," but I ignored it and danced a little faster, a little braver.

A twig snapped.

I stopped. "Is that you, Apollo?" I whispered rashly and grinned at the car. "Come to your maiden queen," I said to the car, extended my arm to it. "Come closer."

I held both arms above my head, swaying them as gracefully as I could in my down jacket, tried to make them look like Ms. Needham's modern dance class. I swayed, bent my body forward, and planted a kiss smack on the hood of the car. Even in the moonlight, I could see the pink imprint clearly. "My love," I said and pressed my lips again on the cool metal. The second lips were lighter than the first. I looked at the lips, my lips on Woolley's car. I pulled my lipstick out of my coat pocket and smeared more onto my lips. "My love," I said again and planted one kiss, two, three more kisses on the hood of Woolley's car. More lipstick and more kisses—I wanted to cover Woolley's face, those lips, those dimples, those eyes with kisses. I continued kissing and calling the car "Woolley dear" and "Woolley darling." I let my lips linger on the white painted surface.

That's when I heard a clear voice in the night: "Stop it. Please stop it!"

That was when a blinding light beamed directly into my eyes from the roof of the garage.

"Don't shine it on her. Don't!" It was Maggie's voice. She grabbed the light from someone—Woolley—and turned it away into the trees. They all sat on the garage roof: Maggie, Woolley, Jack, Roger, Flash, Farrah, Beth, and Larry. They had all been watching me. Watching me dance. Watching me kiss a car. They had heard what I said.

"It was you." Jack's voice sounded far away. His face was colorless.

Maggie cried silently.

Woolley's mouth hung open. "It's Annie," he said.

The others stared.

"It wasn't me. It was Henny," I said. I began rubbing off the lipstick marks but they just made pink smudges. "It wasn't me. This was the first time," I said. "It wasn't me. It was Henny." I fumbled into the car and started it. "It wasn't me," I shouted it and then drove as fast as I'd ever driven through that alley.

"It was Henny," I repeated it all the way home until I was hoarse. "It was Henny."

In the rearview mirror familiar, friendly faces grinned at me: Jack, Woolley, Maggie, Beth, and even Miss Boyle. But their smiles soon distorted to sinister looks, the teeth decayed, the gums diseased, and tongues, forked, darted. The eyes bulged and the clawed hands reached for me to tear me to pieces.

"Don't," I cried. "Please don't." The back of my car coat was torn in shreds. I felt the claws on my skin.

"Don't." I screamed it.

"Wake up, Annie. Wake up." Henny shook my shoulders. "You're having a dream." She sat on the bed. "A nightmare?" she asked. Her face was wan, her hair thin and straggly. She really had been very sick, I realized.

"Yes, I guess I was," I said. My head ached, temples throbbing dully.

"Must have been about monsters," Henny mused, "the way you were moaning and wretching around in your bed." She pulled her robe tighter around her body and shivered slightly. She was so skinny. I'd never noticed how skinny she was before. It made her look vulnerable.

She would hate me when she found out what I'd done. She would hate that I had shared nothing with her, that I had taunted her with her own feelings. Feelings that I shared. I wondered how long it would take Farrah to come over and tell her. A half an hour? Maybe less.

The doorbell rang. Already? Already, she was standing on the front porch waiting for us to answer, chewing her rubbery gum. "You'll never believe where Annie was last night, blah, blah, blah, blah, blah." I pressed the palms of my hands into my eyes and held them there.

"You're crying. What's the matter? Annie?" Henny held

my arm and tried to pull it away from my face. "Annie?" she repeated.

I *was* crying. Tears ran down my face, into my hairline. It was silly, really. I mean, I wouldn't have known I was crying except for the wet on my face, except for Henny's pointing it out to me. I rubbed my face, rubbed it dry.

"It's nothing," I said. "I think I must be getting sick too. I feel so tired." I wanted her to go now and stop being kind to me. I wanted her to be obnoxious again, so I could hate her, so it wouldn't hurt so much when she learned what a cow I was. So it wouldn't hurt when she hated me back.

I listened for Farrah's footsteps through the house to our bedroom. Instead I heard a strange man's voice speaking with Father. And another man's voice. Two men were with Father.

"I wonder who that is." Henny heard them too. She got up. "Be back in a minute," she said.

I closed my eyes and saw the heads of my friends staring down at me from Woolley's garage. Maggie's face, crying. Jack's face. Jack. Had I put that pain there? Was I capable of that? I didn't mean to. It was just my secret. It was just silly fun. I saw Woolley's face. He hardly seemed worth the humiliation now. My face was wet again. Really very wet. I rubbed it. I couldn't stop this silent crying. I must be getting sick, I thought. I must be ill.

"It's the police, and they've found Oma!" Henny's face was now a ghastly white. "She's dead. They've found her, and she's dead!" She ran from the room back downstairs. The two men took turns speaking to Father. I heard the rising and falling of their voices. It was all inaudible.

I got up quickly. The clothes I had worn the night before were piled conveniently on the floor next to the bed. I put them on.

Mother and Father were putting on their coats as I walked

into the dining room. The policemen were now huddled together on the front porch, waiting.

"I want to go too," Henny was saying. "Please let me go."

"Where are you going?" I asked. "Where is Oma?"

"Girls, I want you to stay here." Father's voice was firm but not impatient. "We won't be long." To me, he said, "The police have found a woman's body that fits Oma's description. Your mother and I are going to see if it's her. We won't be long," he said, opening the front door. One of the policemen held the screen open for Mother.

"Where did they find her?" I called to him. I would know if it was Oma from the location. I would know it for certain. They were descending the porch steps behind the policemen. A squad car stood at the curb. It looked alien, parked outside our house.

It was Mother who turned to answer. Her face as sad as any face I'd ever seen. As sad as I felt. "She was lying under Mr. Eberley's porch," she said quietly.

So it *was* Oma.

The funeral was held at Winberry & Siegel Mortuary on South Temple. Father had never attended the Dutch Reformed Church and was perfectly happy to let Bishop Wakefield conduct the funeral in the small chapel.

Before the funeral began, our family was escorted into a small side room where Oma lay in her casket. I don't know why, but this was a surprise to me. I mean I didn't expect to see her dead. I didn't expect ever to see her again, alive or dead. Mother touched Oma's arm. Father stood at her side. Ome Govert and Tante Geert moved down by Oma's feet. Tante Geert cried into her hankie. Henny and I held back a little, and then Henny took my hand and we moved in closer.

"We wanted to have a moment by ourselves, just the family, to say good-bye to Oma," Father said. I could hear the organ begin a prelude in the nearby chapel. I looked down at my new red shoes. They were the most beautiful shoes I'd ever had. They looked good with my gray wool jumper.

There I was, thinking about clothes when I should be thinking about Oma.

"She looks so peaceful," commented Tante Geert. "Just like she's sleeping."

I thought she looked very dead. They had made up her face with an off-color makeup and her hair looked like someone had fixed it who didn't know Oma at all, which was true, of course. Mother noticed it, because she took a comb out of her purse and combed the wave in the front in the opposite direction, where it belonged.

Oma's hands, folded across her abdomen, were crusted with a thick, pasty dark makeup. Her hands, so much like mine, hidden under that crude cover, made me sad. It seemed it had been forever since I had given any thought to Oma. Even when she was gone for those two nights, I didn't much worry. It wasn't my problem what a crazy old lady did. I was not part of her, of her actions, of her craziness, but the hands reminded me that I was. Reminded me of my own craziness. Reminded me of kissing a car in the middle of the night, of four months of crazy, secretive thoughts.

Oma's beautiful hands lay motionless.

A door opened and Bishop Wakefield entered and behind him stood Jack. I looked back at Oma. The room spun around. What were they doing in here?

Father left Mother and shook Bishop Wakefield's hand and then Jack's hand. I only saw it in my peripheral vision. I didn't look directly. I didn't want to see Jack avoid me.

Father cleared his throat. "It's appropriate to have someone say a prayer for the family before the casket is closed, and I have asked Bishop Wakefield to do this. He is not of our faith, but he has been a good neighbor to us, and Jack has been a good friend to Annie and Henny." Father put his arm around Jack's shoulders. Jack smiled briefly at him and then looked down at his feet.

I saw it in my peripheral vision.

Heads bowed and Bishop Wakefield began to pray. I talked to Oma in my head. I'm sorry, Oma, that I didn't pay more attention to you while you were here. I'm sorry that I wasn't kinder, but you were so hard to be kind to sometimes. I'm sorry you were hit by a car. To me you died six years ago, when you changed into that other person.

I am so relieved you are finally gone.

And I am so sorry.

Was it correct for me to be wearing bright red patent leather shoes at my grandmother's funeral? Had I made yet another error in judgment?

Was that Jack who smelled of Old Spice?

Everyone mumbled "Amen," so I knew the prayer had ended. The solicitous man from the mortuary, who seemed to be there whenever we needed him, now stepped forward and began to close the coffin. I looked at Oma's face. It was peaceful. Her hands.

The lid was shut. Someone was crying aloud. It wasn't Mother. It wasn't Henny. It wasn't even Geert. It was me. Mother put her arm around me and patted me with her free arm. "Shh," she whispered.

Tante Geert gave me a dry hanky. "I'm all right," I said. Henny and I followed the adults into the chapel where we were seated on the front pews.

The chapel was filled with people, most of them neighbors, some co-workers of my father and some of my friends, or people who used to be my friends. Maggie sat at the side with her mother and father. Flash sat next to her. The Spivacks sat in the middle somewhere. Mrs. Wakefield, Jack and Milton sat near the front with Mr. Eberley. All of our American neighbors were there. I loved them all like never before.

Even Farrah, who I noticed wasn't chewing gum for once.

Maybe she wouldn't ever tell Henny what I'd done. Maybe Henny would never need to find out that all this year, while I arrogantly put down her affection for Tom Woolley, while I had sneered at her at every opportunity and shown my disgust and my superiority—during all that time, I had been obsessed with him myself. And all that time, when I was pretending to do her a favor by driving her to Woolley's house on Friday nights and getting paid $5.00 each time and threatening to stop, I was actually waiting for Friday to come so that we could go to his house again. What would she say if she knew? What would Henny think of me? It mattered to me what Henny thought. It mattered.

Maybe Farrah would never tell, and I could keep this secret, and my sister would never know what a colossal fraud I was.

The last secret? There would be no more secrets. I would tell Henny myself. I would be honest for once. It would be better coming from me than from Farrah. I would tell her.

The congregation sang, "Come, Ye Disconsolate," but I felt better with my resolve. I looked down at my red shoes. They were even more beautiful than I remembered.

It was awkward having Jack and Maggie at the funeral. "At least I won't have to speak with them. When the funeral is over, they'll go away," I thought to myself. But they didn't go away. Even as we climbed into Ome Govert's Buick station wagon for the procession to the cemetery, I saw Jack and his father get into their Chevrolet and turn the headlights on. They were going to the cemetery too. And later in the cemetery when we were once again praying over Oma's casket, which was set above a neat rectangular hole in the ground, inadequately camouflaged with a sheet of fake grass, I looked up at the group of bowed heads and was confronted with Maggie's stare.

The day was gray, the air wet, although it had stopped

drizzling. "A splendid day for a novel." I wondered if she was thinking the same thing. "I'm truly sorry, Maggie. You're the best friend I ever had, and I'm sorry. What are you thinking?" We didn't drop our gaze. We seemed to be inspecting each other's insides, as if that were possible. Her large brown eyes, unblinking. She was so pretty without her glasses. She was, in fact, beautiful, I realized for the first time. Finally, Dr. Connors, glancing nervously at his watch, pulled on her arm. They nudged through the other people and disappeared into their car.

I gave up trying to stop crying. There seemed nothing I could do about it anyway. So I just let the tears fall. Tante Geert was quick to hand me another hanky. She seemed to be the great supplier.

Jack did not disappear so easily. I was horrified to find him at the buffet luncheon at our house later in the afternoon. His mother had helped with the food and was busying herself back and forth between the dining room and kitchen. Jack kept pretty much with his father, as he had done all morning. I went to a corner of the living room and sat on a folding chair. It felt cold. I was as far away from Jack as I could get.

Mother sat across the room with an old photograph album of Oma's that she showed to Mrs. Spivack and Mr. Eberley.

"She was beautiful and intelligent," said my mother carefully. She didn't practice her English as much as Father.

"Yes she was," agreed Mr. Eberley. He was deeply engrossed in the book and even lifted it from Mother's lap.

Mr. Eberley seemed hypnotized by a picture of Oma in her thirties, wearing the pearls and the silk blouse, looking coolly and confidently into the camera's eye.

"What a waste," he barely breathed it. His white head nodded back and forth. His hands trembled. "What a terrible waste." He closed the book softly and handed it back to Mother and stood up.

"You were very good to her. It couldn't have been easy."

He held Mother's hand in both of his, and then bowed and kissed it.

Mother smiled and whispered thank you. Then spotting me, watching from across the room, Mr. Eberley came to me, reached for my hand and kissed it too. "You were good to her too. I saw you sitting with her on the porch many nights when you probably would rather have been elsewhere."

If you only knew, I thought. You wouldn't smile at me.

He carried his empty plate into the dining room.

And then there was Jack walking toward me with a plate of food and a cup of punch. It must be a mistake, I thought. A hallucination. He doesn't want to talk to me any more than I want to talk to him.

He handed the plate to me. "Mom thought you might like some food," he said. His face was bright red. I had never seen Jack embarrassed about anything before.

"Thanks." I accepted the food, although the thought of eating it made me want to throw up. I felt as red as he looked. He sat in the chair next to me.

"I'm sorry about Oma," he said. He was the only American who referred to her as Oma. "I'll miss her." He looked handsome. He wore the same suit he had worn at the Christmas Dance when we had laughed and sung together.

I sipped the punch not knowing what to say. All I could think of was what he had seen me do four nights ago at Woolley's house. All I could think of was how I had deceived him, how I had lost a good friend in him.

"She liked you," I finally croaked. I cleared my throat. "She really did."

"Well, I don't know if she liked me exactly, but her feelings were consistent anyway." He blushed even brighter.

Did he mean something else?

"No, she liked you," I insisted. There was some kind of tuna salad scent drifting up from the plate on my lap that was nauseating.

He was staring a hole into his black dress shoes.

"I'm glad you came." I realized this was true. Maybe he wouldn't expunge me from his life entirely. Maybe we could play tennis occasionally.

"My father made me." It struck like a blow to the head. He looked up from his shoes and straight into my eyes.

"Oh," I said. It was nothing more than a gasp.

"Good-bye, Annie." He stood up.

"Good-bye, Jack," I said. My body felt so heavy. I wanted to slump into a heap on the carpet.

He was gone. I was sure he would never speak to me again.

I couldn't sit in the room another second. I carried the plate into the kitchen, set it on the table with the dirty dishes, and walked directly into the bathroom, locking the door behind me. I sat on the rim of the tub and began to sob out loud—too loud for all the people in the house who might hear me. I buried my face into one of the towels and continued sobbing. For the first time I began to wish I was back in Utrecht. I pulled my face out of the towel and saw my reflection in the mirror. My face was puffed up and splotchy and ugly. I cried again into the towel. Somebody knocked on the door, a soft tentative knock.

"Just a minute," I said. "I'll be out in just a minute."

"I'll come back," said the female voice.

I folded the towel back onto the rack. I couldn't stay there. It wasn't safe. I decided to go to bed. I would say I was sick. I could do that. They wouldn't bother me with anything, just try to feed me once in a while and then let me sleep. That's what I wanted most was sleep. I wanted to be unconscious. My limbs were so heavy and so weak. I could hardly turn the doorknob. I slipped down the hall and into my room, closing the door behind me.

But I wasn't alone. Henny sat Indian-style on her bed, with

149

Farrah half sprawled across the foot of the bed. They both turned to look at me.

"You look terrible," Farrah said with her usual directness.

"I don't feel well," I said. That was true enough. "Would you two mind going somewhere else? I'd like to go to bed."

Farrah made a move to get up, but Henny held her leg down.

"No, we don't want to go anywhere else," Henny said. Her face looked challenging. "Feel free to go to bed anyway, though," she continued. Her lips pressed tightly together when she finished speaking.

Farrah had told her. I could barely hold my head up, it was so heavy. I sat on my bed and removed my shoes. Henny and Farrah watched me without saying anything. I reached back, unzipped my jumper and pulled it over my head laying it in a soft lump on my shoes. My nightgown was not under my pillow where it usually was and rather than walk across the room to the chest of drawers to get another one, I got into bed. Henny and Farrah were silent. I turned my face to the wall and pulled the blankets up as far as I could without actually pulling them over my head.

"Well, like I said, Farrah, I think I've made a complete fool of myself this year following Tom Woolley around as if he were a god, an *Apollo.*" She rolled the "l's" languidly with her tongue.

She knew.

"Annie said I was oversexed and crude. Didn't you, Annie dear?" She paused and waited for a reply. I had my eyes shut as tight as possible. Let her think I was asleep. I go to sleep fast. Let her think it, please.

"Annie's been very good all year about pointing out my character faults to me, especially when it comes to boys. I'm always doing it wrong. I'm much too aggressive, she told me."

"Come on Henny, let's go to my house." I could hear

shifting on the bed. This conversation made even Farrah nervous.

"It's too bad that you don't have a sister like mine to set an example for you—a refined, restrained, perfect sort of girl. You must envy me that."

"Henny, I'm going home. Come with me now."

"I want to be with my sweet sister, but thank you anyway."

More rustling noises and steps to the door. "See ya tomorrow," Farrah said.

"See ya."

The door closed.

"You're not asleep, you witch!" Henny grasped the bedding and pulled it back off the bed.

"Don't," I said making a feeble attempt to rescue my covers. "Don't do that. Please, I'm sick."

"Poor baby." She pinched my cheek. "Poor little baby."

"Henny, please . . ."

"All this time you were criticizing me for being boy crazy and silly. You were so high and mighty about it. So pompous, so unforgiving. So very snotty." Her face was so close to mine that she spit on me with the word "snotty." "I even began to believe you. Began to think there was something wrong with *me*. That *I* was sick. You snot. You creepy, whiny snot. I hate you." She shoved me with both hands and I hit my head against the wall.

"All year long you were feeling exactly what I was feeling. Then you blamed me! You sneaky snot. You wanted me to keep it a secret, and then when you're caught, you blame me! You witch! But they didn't believe you. That's irony for you." Her fist pounded my shoulder. "It wasn't enough for you to have Jack Wakefield all tied up. You wanted something better. Did you sneak in here at night and kiss the pictures above my bed? Maybe you prayed to them. Maybe you called them mythical names and danced the dance of the seven toilet-paper streams." She kept hitting me around the shoulders. "Maybe you took your clothes off and . . ."

"Stop it." I hit her as hard as I could on the arm. "Stop it," I screamed at her.

"Why was it so important that I never see this side of you? Why did it have to be such a dark secret, Miss Snot Face?" She pulled on my hair.

"I'll tell you why. Because if you had told me that would have made us equal, but as long as you kept it a secret you could be Miss Superior Snot." She pinched my cheek again, hard. "Miss Scum," she hissed.

I slapped her face as hard as I could. She thumped a coiled fist on my back. "You're just a liar," she puffed. She never stopped hitting. "You've always been a liar. You've always hidden things—not just secrets, but cookies and candy. You hide them in your pillow case. You're a snake. You lie to make Mother and Father think you're wonderful, mature, everything a good daughter should be, and you blame me for everything. You've never sided with me. No one in this family ever sides with me. I thought you were beginning to side with me. I thought we had a secret. But you had the real secret. You had the real secret!" She was crying too, but she still pounded her fists onto my back and shoulders. And I pounded mine back on her until I noticed blood on my arm and realized my nose was bleeding.

"My nose . . ."

"Your precious nose is bleeding again. You must be experiencing stress." She had my head in a headlock with one arm and with the other she rubbed the palm of her hand under my nose and spread the blood on my face. "I almost weakened with you, Annie. I thought we were going to be real sisters." Her face was next to mine. I could feel her hot breath. She sobbed as she talked. The blood streamed from my nose and onto my slip.

152

"I'll never make that mistake again." She pushed me back. I hit my head against the wall.

"Witch," she shouted and slammed the door behind her.

We did not fight in my family. My father and mother expected their daughters to act like ladies. In fact one of the reasons my father decided to come to America is because he thought Holland had become "a pisspot of pornography" and no place for "nice girls." My mother had a serene spirit and almost never raised her voice. When she was young, she too had been a nice girl. Our Oma, whose face was once smooth and fair, and who had worn fox furs around her long lovely neck with the little fox head in tact, was raised in a European city where Rembrandt himself had walked. She was a lady to her tiny earlobes. She was a lady until a car ran her down, the precious fox furs spinning into someone's bicycle spokes. After that she was a nuisance and no lady.

We did not fight in my family. Except once. My sister Henny and I beat on each other in our bedroom while in the living room friends and relatives gathered to mourn the passing of my grandmother, who ran away from home and died under a neighbor's porch. We fought, and while my sister had me in a headlock, I bit her finger. Later I found out it was broken.

I didn't go to school for three weeks, but lay in bed. I wanted to sleep, to be unconscious as much as possible. My parents thought I suffered from some mystical stress connected to Oma's death.

I didn't see Henny at all. She had moved into Oma's room downstairs. Mother moved her clothes out of the closet and told me about Henny's broken finger that she had mashed in the bathroom door. I never saw it. Mother also removed the masking tape from the center of the room and made Henny's bed, or what used to be Henny's bed. More than anything, the bed all made up neatly, the pillow in its place, erased Henny from the room. She almost never made her bed. I missed her. She had spoken the truth, and I recognized it. I did have to be number one in the family. I wanted to feel superior to Henny. I never wanted to admit that my feelings were the same as hers, when they were exactly the same.

I missed Maggie and Jack. I was sure I would never have friends again.

At the end of the third week, Father, not Mother, brought my dinner on a tray. He sat on my bed and watched me eat for a while. When he finally did talk, he said, "Monday I want you to go back to school."

I set the plate of food down on the blankets. I was terrified of going back. I couldn't face seeing Woolley, Flash, Beth— all of them. I didn't want to see Jack look away from me as if we had never kissed with chocolate in our mouths. I didn't want Maggie staring at me like she didn't know who I was.

"Please no," I pleaded with my father. "I'm not ready yet."

"Yes," he said firmly. "Tomorrow is Saturday, and I want you to get up and get dressed. I want you out of this bed. I'm afraid you'd stay here the rest of your life if we let you."

"Please, just a little while longer." I wiped the tears with my hands.

"I don't know what's troubling you," Father said. "I can't make your sadness go away, but you will have to live with the sadness outside of this bed." He stroked my head. "Do you understand?"

I nodded.

"Tomorrow you will get up."

"Yes."

In the morning, I got dressed. More than anything I was afraid of having Henny spit a streaming, sarcastic monologue of my sins at me through breakfast. In the mirror I saw my gray face, the oily, flat hair hung limp on my shoulders. I went downstairs.

The kitchen looked strange and brighter than I remembered it. Mother had replaced the vinyl cloth with a white cloth.

"Good morning," she said when I walked in. She stood at the stove making pancakes. I sat down in my place across from Henny, who looked at her plate.

"How do you feel?" Father asked.

"Better," I lied.

Henny looked up from her plate. There was a moment of shock when she looked into my face. "Maggie has been asking about you," she said, her face very controlled. "She didn't want to bother you, but she wanted to know how you were."

"Really?" I was immensely grateful for this information. I tried smiling.

She looked back at her plate.

I wondered if she regretted our fight as much as I did. I regretted the whole fall. She was my sister. I wished I hadn't taken that for granted. I missed her.

Mother chatted happily through breakfast. It seemed odd not to have her fussing about Oma. She was like a new person. "I'm going to take driving lessons," she announced.

It took all my energy to find things to do for the rest of the weekend. More than anything, I wanted to go to bed, to sleep. I played the piano and read short stories out of the *Ladies' Home Journal.* Once I walked over to the Safeway to buy some bread for Mother, both dreading and hoping to see Jack, but I didn't. In the afternoon, the mailman brought a thick letter from Kaatje. I went to my bedroom to open it. As I unfolded the onionskin, several snapshots spilled out onto the bedspread. I picked them up: pictures of Edo's wedding. I looked at them carefully. They seemed like figures out of a dream in their formal dress. The picture of Kaatje, her dark short hair framed with a wide-brimmed hat, the dark eyes smiling, made me cry again. Would I never stop crying? My only friend in the whole world and she was only six thousand miles away. I wrote her the briefest note, thanking her for the pictures, telling her of Oma's death and that I'd been sick and how I was very glad that she was really and truly coming to visit me this summer. The problem is, I thought to myself, how am I going to survive until then?

On Monday I returned to school. In first period Woolley said, "Hi, Annie, glad you're back," as if nothing had ever happened. He just plunked his handsome body down in front of me. Beth was more shy about it, but she said "hi" too. Nobody wanted to talk about it, but then, neither did I.

Only Jack did not speak or look at me. He sat rigid in the seat next to mine and when the bell rang, he hurried out.

Miss Boyle greeted me when I walked into choir and whisked me into her office to ask me if I could be one of the accompanists for the *Pajama Game* rehearsals. "We'll spend class time on it, of course, but it will require a lot of after school time too." Maggie was the other accompanist, of course. Could I come after school tonight for the tryouts? "Kids come to try out with sheet music, but no pianist," she said. "You and Maggie can trade off."

I told her I'd do it. It was a wonderful way to keep busy, and that's what I wanted was to keep busy. It was another way of being unconscious.

The bell rang, and the chatter in the adjoining choir room became a humming A note.

"They're flat," muttered Miss Boyle as we walked toward the door. "By the way, are you feeling better? I didn't even ask you. You were gone a long time."

"A lot better," I said. "Thanks."

Maggie met us as we crossed into the choir room. She wore the Irish knit sweater Mac had sent her for Christmas.

156

"Miss Boyle," she whispered. The three of us stood in front of the whole choir. I longed to look for Jack in the bass section. "Could I talk to Annie in your office for just a few minutes? It's real important."

Miss Boyle nodded, already she had her arm raised, her index finger pointing at the ceiling trying to get the choir to raise the A. She hit the A on the piano. They were a quarter of a pitch off.

Maggie pushed me into Miss Boyle's office and closed the door. We stood in front of Miss Boyle's desk, which was covered with papers and sheet music. "I wanted to talk to you first thing. I don't want to lose my nerve," she said taking a deep breath. "First of all," she breathed deeply again, "I want to tell you how sorry I am about what we did. I mean, how we spied on you." Her chin trembled.

"You don't have to, Maggie. It was my fault," I said.

She put her hand up to stop me. "No, I have to," she said firmly. "I'm very ashamed. We all thought it would be fun, and we had no idea who it would be—it was so terrible!" She pulled a Kleenex out of the box on Miss Boyle's desk and held on to it.

"It was my fault," I said again.

"Let me finish," Maggie insisted. Her eyes were not even slightly crossed with the new contact lenses. She swept her hair back with an impatient gesture. "I'm ashamed I didn't come to talk to you when you were sick or say anything to you at your grandmother's funeral—" She wiped her eyes with the Kleenex, "but I was angry." She looked straight into my eyes, her fist clutching the Kleenex. "And I was hurt that you hadn't told me anything. Nothing. I thought I was your best friend. I shared everything with you and you have this whole secret life that I don't know anything about." She grabbed more Kleenex and hid her face for a moment. "I thought you liked Jack!" she said from behind the tissues. She wiped her face and bit her lip.

157

"I did—I do like Jack," I said. "It's so hard to explain." I sat on a bench near the door. Maggie sat next to me. "When I saw Woolley on the first day of school, I was just blown away! He was so handsome, so perfect, and everything he said was what I wanted to hear. You know what I mean?"

She nodded her head. At least she was smiling.

"There's more . . ." I hesitated. "Woolley reminded me of Edo Tefsen. I'd had a crush on him since I was twelve!"

"Kaatje's brother, right?"

I nodded. "And just before school started, I learned that Edo was getting married. I always thought that *I* would marry Edo. I just assumed I'd grow up and marry Edo. And then I realized that my plan to marry him was just a fantasy—something I'd made up in my head and I decided never to deceive myself that way again, until that first day in Mr. Crow's class and Woolley walked in the door. That was only *weeks* later. Only weeks and I was living fantasies all over again. I was so ashamed to feel that way," I continued. "You remember how Henny and Farrah talked about Woolley all summer long? Remember how disgusted we were with them? And there I was acting just like Henny and Farrah. I didn't want to be like them. And yet, he was there every morning, smelling wonderful, smiling at me, tantalizing me. He's very handsome—like Edo, and he's charming."

Maggie nodded, "Yes, he is," she agreed.

"I wanted to kiss the back of his neck. Seriously!"

She laughed out loud.

"I actually weighed in my mind if it was worth it to place a big smack on that neck right there in Mr. Crow's English class. I really wanted to do it."

Maggie smiled. "You had the hots," she said.

"I hate that expression," I said. "It's so crude."

"You had the hots," she repeated.

"I did," I said. "I had them bad."

Outside the wind blew a leafless branch against the window. It made a scraping noise.

"Remember when Henny kissed him during the assembly, behind the piano. You and I were sitting right there. We nearly gagged to death. She was so out of control. I was so ashamed to be related to her, and at the same time, at the very same time, I was so jealous of her for just taking what she wanted, even if it was behind the piano!"

Maggie laughed again. "You really did have them bad." She smiled.

"I thought you'd be so disgusted with me. I thought you'd think I was just like Henny. I was so disgusted myself. And it didn't make any sense!" I hit my fist on my knee. "I was dating Jack, who I really liked—who I still like." My face wobbled.

Maggie got up and picked the Kleenex box off Miss Boyle's desk. "Here, take the whole box," she said placing the box in my lap. She sat next to me again, one arm around my heaving shoulders. "I never would have thought you were like Henny or Farrah. I still don't. Losing Jack is something to cry over, though," she sighed. So I cried for a long time. Maggie joined in, both of us using Kleenexes like blotters until the bottom of Miss Boyle's wastepaper can was covered with them. In the other room, the choir sang "Waters Ripple and Flow." The words about a faithless lover floated through the door. Oh, Jack.

The music stopped, and the door opened. Miss Boyle stood in the doorway, stared at us, said "Oh," and shut the door again. Maggie and I dabbed at our faces and laughed. "She looks like a choir leader without an accompanist." Maggie giggled. "Let's cut class. We look too terrible to go in. I'll write her a note." She scribbled a note and placed it in Miss Boyle's chair.

"Let's go walking," I said. "I'll tell you every gruesome,

hideous detail of my late fantasy life. Are we still friends?" I asked. I wanted to be certain, to hear it from her lips.

"The very best," she said.

Ms. Needham was sympathetic about my long illness and let me study the rules for basketball while the other girls played it. Mr. Dayton gave me a couple of chapters of algebra to complete. It would take me three times as long now that Jack wouldn't be available to help me with it. Ms. Humphries was annoyed that I'd been sick. She told me several times that there was simply no way I could make up the labs. I didn't beg. I really didn't care about her stupid labs. I stood silently while she decided what I *could* do to make up for the long absence. Finally she said I could take the term final on Friday. I thanked her and sat in my seat next to Larry, who seemed a little embarrassed to have to sit so close to me: the obsessed toilet paper freak. Or maybe that was only my imagination. I would have to stay up every single night to catch up on the homework for physiology alone, and I still had to finish the paper on *Macbeth* for English as well as the volumes of algebra. I rested my head in my hand and tried to keep the headache from pressing down on my eyes.

"Annie Sehlmeier!" Ms. Humphries's sharp voice rose to where I sat. "Are you sleeping?"

I sat up straight. "No ma'am," I said quickly. I almost saluted. It seemed like the natural thing to do.

"Well, see that you don't." She kept her evil eye on me for several long seconds and then turned back to the board.

Larry leaned over to me. "At least she didn't throw chalk at you." He smiled.

I nodded at him. I felt incredibly grateful that he'd spoken to me.

Mr. Benson told me that anyone who had been sick for almost a month should not have to worry about U.S. history and refused to give me any makeup work. "You've been an A student up to now, no reason for me to think that you've stopped being one," he said, gently nudging me to my seat. I wanted to cry out of gratitude but didn't.

After school Maggie and I sat in the front row of the auditorium listening to tryouts for *Pajama Game*. Several students dotted the auditorium to listen to their friends. Sometimes Maggie or I would move to the piano to play for someone who didn't have an accompanist, but most kids brought a friend to play for them. Beth Knabe's voice wobbled nervously, and her neck splotched so badly you could probably see it from the back row of the balcony.

"Thanks very much, Beth," Miss Boyle called cheerfully from the middle of the orchestra seats. She called Henny's name. Mr. Charest, the orchestra leader, sat next to her. I shifted nervously in my seat. My stomach flipflopped. Henny walked center stage as if she owned the place.

"She certainly looks confident!" Maggie whispered.

Farrah sat at the piano arranging the sheet music. With a nod from Henny she began the introduction of "Steam Heat," making several mistakes as she went.

"Why didn't Henny have you play?" Maggie asked.

"We're not speaking, remember?"

"Oh yes."

Henny began, her voice strong and energetic, but she had to stop when Farrah lost her place. They began again. Henny was such a surprise. I mean I'd heard her at home, belting out popular songs—I knew she could sing—but she was so relaxed there in the auditorium, snapping her fingers and swaying her hips, just as if she were in our dining room.

Farrah, who seemed under overwhelming pressure, lost her place again. Henny looked understandably irritated.

I moved to the piano. "Why don't you let me play it," I said gently, nudging Farrah off the bench.

"Gladly," she whispered.

Henny nodded at me and I started the introduction, trying to match my playing style with Henny's singing style. Henny

161

smiled, snapped her fingers. She sizzled the words and looked provocatively down at Miss Boyle, who nodded her head in rhythm. The piano wailed along. Sing to the back row, Henny, I thought. I saw SEHLMEIER SISTERS flashing in neon lights before my eyes.

When she was done, a couple of "wows" came out of the house seats, and everyone clapped. Henny, true to form, blew them kisses and bowed dramatically before skimming off the stage. Miss Boyle and Mr. Charest exchanged glances, Mr. Charest raising his eyebrows as if to say, "Well, well, well." Henny played the flute in his orchestra.

Henny padded down the stage steps by the piano, her face flushed with success.

"Thanks for playing," she said. She touched my arm timidly.

"You were wonderful," I said. "You were perfect."

"You made it easier," she said.

"I'm glad, Henny. I really am."

I got home before Henny and found the masking tape in the garage. I ran a line of it across the center of Henny's bedroom floor, which was surprisingly tidy, up the walls and then drew a sign with a magic marker that read, "I'll stay on any side of the tape you want, but can we be sisters? Love, Insufferable Annie."

Mother sent me to the Safeway for lettuce. When I returned, I found a line of masking tape through my own bedroom with a note in Henny's scrawl: "Let's make the tape a symbol of past separations. I want us to be sisters too. I've missed you. Love, Obnoxious Henny. P.S. I have two Twinkies hidden in my pillow case. Meet me at 8:00—my room. P.P.S. Thanks again for helping me this afternoon."

My body stopped feeling so heavy after I made up with Maggie and Henny. Going to bed in the daytime wasn't so attractive anymore, but late at night, after a long day of school and rehearsals and homework, I collapsed onto the mattress and fell asleep with my clothes on.

Henny got the female comedy lead in *Pajama Game.* She rehearsed every waking minute. We were both busier than we had ever been before. I was grateful for the busyness. It kept my mind off Jack, who continued ignoring me entirely. I thought of writing him a note, trying to explain how I could like him and Tom Woolley at the same time, but I could hardly explain it to myself. Besides I felt a note would embarrass him somehow. I longed to have him even as a casual friend, but he refused to look at me, let alone speak to me.

Maggie told me on the way home from school one afternoon that Jack had asked her to go out with him after the first performance of *Pajama Game,* which was a few days away.

"I told him I'd tell him tomorrow," she said. She drove the green Volvo down the steepest part of 8th South. The sun in the west, directly in front of us, was a deep orange. "I know you still like Jack—a lot." She paused. "And I don't want to be disloyal. Jack and I are only friends. He's Mac's friend, you know." She flipped the sun visor down onto the window.

I sighed. "Jack is not ever going to ask me anywhere again. I know that. If he doesn't ask you, he'll take someone else. It makes no difference. It really doesn't." I felt like I'd been shot at close range through the chest. If things had happened differently, he would have asked me, and we would laugh and talk and kiss under the yellow porch light of my house until Father signaled for me to come in.

I miss you, Jack, I thought. How long will it take before I stop missing you?

"Are you sure?" Maggie parked in front of my house.

"I'm absolutely sure. I'm also a little envious." I opened the door and pulled out my back pack. "I'm going in to

163

commit suicide," I said and grinned at her like the proverbial good sport. My insides ached.

"Gas or gun?" Maggie smiled.

"Oreo overdose."

"That's the worst!"

I closed the door. She honked as she drove off.


In the house, I studied my face in the bathroom mirror. I saw it then: saw that I didn't look like Meryl Streep at all except for the long blond hair. "May I borrow the car for about an hour?" I asked Mother, who was mixing meatballs in a bowl. Father hadn't come home yet.

"We're going to eat soon," she said, breaking eggs into the bowl.

"Just an hour, please," I begged.

"For an hour only," she said.

I drove to 9th South and parked the car in front of the Tower Theater. I walked in to the Fashionette Salon next door to the theater. The place smelled of disguised ammonia, of permanents and hair dye. Black and white tiles covered the floors and the walls were papered in white with parrot green trellises.

"May I help you?" the woman behind the desk asked.

"I want to have my hair cut and blown dry. Is there anyone available right now?" I knew it was a risk to walk in off the street and ask for the generic "anyone," but I needed right away to look as little like Meryl Streep as possible. And besides, "anyone" could cut it better than I could do it myself, and I felt almost that desperate.

The woman turned and called, "Angie, can you stay for one more cut and blow?" She turned back to me. "It's almost closing time," she said.

Angie yelled "yeah," from the back, but when she came to the front and saw the length of my hair, she blew air out of her mouth, "Whew, you mean a real hair cut, don't you? How short do you want it?" she asked me.

"Very short." I said. "Not past my ear."

"Bangs? Feathered, what?"

"Yes," I said, following her to a room in the back. "No," I said. "I want a new bob and no bangs." I had seen that in a magazine somewhere. I had no idea if I would look any good in it.

Angie washed and dried my hair, wrapped me in a huge plastic cape and swiveled my chair so that I faced the mirror. She combed my hair out long and straight. "Are you sure about this? You're going to be losing a lot of hair. Does your mother know?"

"Of course," I lied. I figured it was none of her business.

She sighed an unsure sigh and began clipping a little tentatively at first. "Oh laws," she said as long strands of hair fell off my shoulder. "Oh laws, I hope you've thought about this. It'll take years to grow it as long as you had it."

"You're doing a nice job," I said, trying to encourage her to continue.

It made her laugh. "Thanks a heap," she snorted.

I watched my new head emerge in the mirror. My neck seemed longer and my face looked fuller and healthier. I began to get excited about this new me. "I like it," I couldn't help saying aloud.

Angie looked at me in the mirror. "I like it too," she said. "You have some natural curl, did you know that?" She began blowing it with the hair dryer and shaping it with a round prickly brush. I watched impatiently in the mirror. It was going to look good, no, great. I could see it was going to look just great. "It's fantastic!" I said when she was finished.

"You lucked out," she said. "I'll bet you decided to do this about the time you were driving past the place. Right?" She wrapped the electric cord around the hair dryer and put it in a drawer.

165

"No, about five minutes earlier than that." I laughed.

"I thought so." She handed me a card. "You'll need a trim about once a month," she said. "You're lucky you got me. I'm the best cutter they've got." She whispered this although we were now entirely alone in the shop.

"I'm glad I got you too then," I said. I paid her. "I feel like a new person," I said. I couldn't help giggling.

"Sometimes that's necessary," she said and waved me out the door.

Father, Mother, and Henny stopped eating dinner when I stepped in through the back door. Their mouths hung open in unified surprise. "How do you like the new me?" I asked.

"Annie!" Mother was in shock.

"Wow!" This was Henny.

"Is that a new shirt?" my father asked, returning to his dinner.

I smiled at him and sat down in my chair.

"I really like it," said Henny. "I mean, I really really like it. It's you," she said.

"I can't believe it," said Mother.

"It's a good-looking shirt," said Father.

"It's the new me," I said.

"The new you looks pretty good," said Father.

"Yes, it does look good," said Mother, rallying. "It looks very nice. Really."

"It looks fantastic," said Henny.

"To the new Annie!" Father raised his water glass and clinked it heartily against Henny's glass, spilling water. "May she be as happy as the old Annie once was." He drank some water, rose from his seat and came over and kissed my cheek.

"I'm trying," I said. "I'm really trying."

Henny was a total sensation in *Pajama Game.* One of her fans was the ever-fickle Tom Woolley, who invited her for pizza

166

after opening night, and Henny had the "delicious pleasure" as she put it, to turn him down, because, of course, she was going with Roger. They went with Maggie and Jack, Beth and Larry. I watched the late movie, *The Way We Were,* with Robert Redford and Barbra Streisand and cried my eyes out.

Another of Henny's fans was Father. He was simply astonished with Henny's talent. "She was really good," he kept saying when he got home. "She was the very best one, don't you think, Riet?" He nudged Mother, who sat on the sofa next to him. "You know, my father used to sing and act in his youth. She probably got it from him," Father said.

"I'm sure her talent comes from *your* side of the family," Mother drawled.

Father grinned apishly. "When she's good, she's mine. When she's bad, she's yours," he chuckled, "heh, heh, heh."

This was the first time I had heard Father really like something that Henny did. And I didn't feel jealous.

Maggie continued seeing Jack through the spring. Most of it was casual dates, sundaes after church at the Garden Gate, tennis at Liberty Park, sometimes a movie. Maggie talked freely about their times together without my having to ask her. I think she knew I wouldn't. She would say, "I told Jack that you and I had tried bicycling through Emigration Canyon and almost killed ourselves," or "I told Jack about our goal to read all the Jane Austen novels before graduation." It was as if she were trying to make sure that he not forget that I still existed. It was also as if she needed to remind me that she had no romantic expectations with Jack. I wondered finally, if having a friendship with both him and me, juggling it as she seemed to be doing, wasn't getting tiresome for her. I hoped it wasn't. I enjoyed hearing any bit of news about Jack that I could get.

In April, Maggie was a bridesmaid for her cousin Brenda's wedding. She made her own dress, a long, pale pink taffeta gown with a ruffled top and bottom. "I feel like Little Bo

Peep," she said, standing in front of the mirror on her closet door in her bedroom.

"You look great," I said. It was true. Her hair was thick and dark, parted to one side. It fell forward when she looked down at her hem. She pushed it back as automatically as she had once pushed the glasses back on the bridge of her nose.

I sat on the carpet folding back the edge of the hem. "Here?" I said.

"Yes, I want it over the back of my heel, just barely, though. I saw Jack last night," Maggie said.

"Turn," I said.

"He's going to Stanford. He got a full scholarship."

I pulled the pins out of my mouth. "Really?" I looked at her face in the mirror. She nodded her head, pushing her hair back of her ear. "He did it. Isn't that great? It's what he wanted," I said. "I think it's terrific." I would not be able to tell him so. "Turn a little," I said, getting back to the pinning.

Maggie straightened up and turned.

"We talked about you the whole evening."

"Some date," I said casually, but my antenna was out, waiting. "Turn just a little."

Maggie shuffled her feet. "He was really thrown by that night at Woolley's. He said it was like he didn't know you, and he was embarrassed and humiliated." She paused. "And mad as a grizzly."

"All those good emotions," I said.

Maggie turned without my asking. We had a rhythm going now. She stood with her back to the mirror, craned her neck around to look. "Cover the heels slightly," she reminded me.

"Then what?" I prodded. I couldn't stand it.

"I told him I had felt the same way."

I groaned.

"And," she continued, "he wanted to know how I'd been able to make up with you so quickly."

"He asked that?"

"Then I told him everything you told me that first day when you came back to school."

"Everything?"

"Everything, including all that stuff about Edo, and I told him that you missed him."

"Did he believe that?"

"I don't know. It's true. I thought he should hear it."

I put the last pin into place and sat on the bed, Indian-style.

Maggie twisted back and forth in front of the mirror, scrutinizing the hem and then admiring herself.

"I'm glad he knows," I said, stretching out on the bed.

"Well, I gave him an earful. Don't know what he'll do with it though." She unzipped the dress and carefully lifted it over her head.

"Maybe, he'll forgive me," I said. It felt like a prayer.

The following Monday, before the bell in first period, Jack sat down in his seat next to mine and said, "Hi, Annie."

I was stunned. "Hi," I returned. I had a mammoth frog in my throat.

"How have you been?"

"Okay." I cleared my throat.

Woolley sat down in front of me, turned around and said, "Hi Annie Piannie," a name he invented during the musical rehearsals. There was something so guileless about him. Not once had he hinted of what I had done. For that, a part of me would always love him.

Jack looked amusedly at Woolley. "Piannie?" he quoted.

"As in player," Woolley said.

"Your literary gifts astonish me."

"Even you, Stanford, class of '91? I'm flattered." Woolley's eyes followed Beth to her seat next to him. "Great duds," he cooed across the aisle. Beth wore a new yellow jump suit. "Will you marry me, beautiful Beth?" He pursed his lips.

"As soon as you return the three dollars you owe me." She

169

leaned down to his face. "Handsome is as handsome does," she said. "Fork it over. It's my lunch money." She held the palm of her hand out. Woolley searched in his pockets and began dropping small change into it.

Jack watched me. "I got into Stanford," he said.

"I know. Maggie told me. I'm really glad. I mean," I stammered, "it's just great."

"I'm pretty happy about it myself." He grinned.

"He's not going to speak to any of us when he returns. He'll be so smart." Beth settled into her seat with her money.

"I'll speak." He said it to me. Then he turned to Beth and imitating Woolley said, "Even to you, beautiful Beth."

She giggled and, as the bell rang and Mr. Crow appeared, she dropped several quarters onto the floor.

Woolley recovered three, leaned across the aisle and whispered, "How about a kiss for seventy-five cents?"

After that Jack always spoke. He honked as he drove by the house when I sat on the porch, but he never stopped. Henny noticed that he was more cordial again.

"Did you and Jack make up?" she asked after he had driven by and waved. We sat on the wooden steps after dinner watching the sky turn crimson. The playing field across the street was absolutely bare.

"He speaks to me. Maggie negotiated some kind of truce," I said. "It's much better than before. Much."

"Do you love Jack?" It was an earnest question. She leaned against the porch post and waited for my answer.

"I honestly don't know," I said. "I haven't the vaguest notion of what love is. Do you love Roger?" I asked. They had been dating steadily since the Christmas Dance.

"I like to kiss him." She laughed. "A lot." She bit her lip. "I don't think that's necessarily love, though."

"Well," I said. "The imitation is pretty heady stuff, if you ask me." I sighed. I felt as old as Oma. "And it doesn't feel that bad either." I began to laugh about the whole horrible winter.

"It sure doesn't," Henny agreed. "And we should know!" She whispered it. We both guffawed.

Mother stood behind the screen door. "What are you two laughing about?" she asked. "It sounds pretty raucous out here."

"Love," I said.

"What's so funny about that?" She waved a fly away from her face. "I don't think love is so funny," she said.

"That's what's so funny," Henny said.

I nodded. We both laughed again.

# PART 6

## *Graduation*

B ECAUSE Jack spoke to me, I nourished a faint hope that he would ask me to the graduation dance. He seemed entirely relaxed around me again, chatted easily about his family and often walked with me to choir after English. I told him about the scholarship to the University of Utah that I had received for the fall. "It's not as good as Stanford," I said.

"It's great," he said.

But it was Maggie he asked, not me.

"He was waiting at my locker after seventh period," she said. We walked down 8th South loaded with full back packs, shopping bags of silver paper and glitter for cutout stars, and miles of cheesecloth for decorations for the dance. "I thought he would ask you," she continued.

"He's been dating you all spring," I said. "Asking you to the graduation dance should be no surprise." I was reminding myself more than her.

"I'm pretty sure Mac asked him to take me. He's been stewing in his letters that he wouldn't be here to take me himself. Maybe someone will still ask you. I want you to be there." She stomped her foot.

"No prospects in sight." I sighed. I fought the heaviness I felt in my limbs.

We waited at the intersection for several cars to pass by and crossed the street.

"Why don't you come anyway? You could help with refreshments and . . ."

"Maggie," I stalled on the sidewalk. "Do you mean to tell me that if you didn't have a date to the graduation dance, you'd go alone and pour punch?"

She ran the toe of her shoe across a crack in the sidewalk and sighed. "I guess I wouldn't."

"Right," I said.

"What are you going to do?"

"Make stars," I said.

Making stars is exactly what I did and I sewed what seemed like a thousand yards of cheesecloth together to make a false ceiling. A week before graduation I thought of an idea to build a gazebo for the center of the dance floor, where the orchestra would sit. The dance committee thought it a great idea, including Ms. Needham, who was our faculty adviser, but she wondered if there was time to complete it. I said I would take care of it. Anything to keep busy. Anything to avoid that heavy feeling of wanting to sleep and avoid my life.

I drew up a plan, bought the lumber, and helped Father nail it together one night at the school. Henny, Beth, Maggie, and I painted it on the day of commencement with a fast-drying acrylic paint. Maggie and Beth both had hair appointments because of the dance, so Henny and I put the finishing touches on the gazebo. It looked stunning.

"I'm a genius," I said, admiring the finished product. Henny was stuffing scraps into a plastic garbage bag.

"I admire your modesty," Henny drawled.

"I don't feel like being modest today," I said. "If I had a date to the dance, I could afford to be modest, but I don't."

The room was all white and silver. The gazebo waited for the orchestra.

I'm glad this is the end of it, I thought. I'm glad high school is over. Next fall Jack will be gone to Palo Alto, and I'll be here at the university with my other friends—a whole new life. This year will have passed away like a short sneeze.

Henny and I turned off the lights and walked to the doors, our footsteps echoing in the oversized hall. *Good-bye, East High,* I thought.

At home, I barely had time to shower and change for dinner. Mother had invited Ome Govert and Tante Geert to eat with us and go to commencement. I heard them shouting for "the graduate" while I blew my hair dry.

"I'm coming," I called.

"Ah, she is beautifying herself," I heard Ome Govert say through the door.

I brushed my hair carefully and then looked critically at myself in the mirror. I wore a soft two-piece dress Mother had made copying a Laura Ashley design with a belt of seashells that Henny had picked out for me. My short hair was perfect—probably because I didn't have a date.

"You look better than Meryl Streep," I muttered to my reflection.

Dinner was cheerful. I couldn't help thinking how different it would be if Oma were still there. Tante Geert sat in Oma's place next to me. Occasionally she would hug me or pinch my face. "I'm so proud of you, Annie," she would gush. I thought of how generous she had always been with me, and how I had always rebuffed her affections. I knew she thought of me like a daughter. After dessert and champagne toasts I stood up and hugged her around the neck. "Thank you for coming," I said. "I really appreciate it." She was so grateful, she practically suffocated me into her fat grasp, but I wasn't sorry I'd said it.

The commencement was held in a large hall on the university campus a few miles from our house to accommodate all the extra guests of the graduates. I had to be there early to warm up with the senior choir, so Henny drove me up in Ome Govert's Buick and went back to get the others.

I met Maggie in a room adjoining the auditorium, where we put on our caps and gowns. The girls wore white and the boys red—our school colors.

Maggie faced me. "This is it!" She flipped the tassel of my mortar board playfully.

"Thank heaven," I said.

I followed her into the hall and through the opened doors of the auditorium. Miss Boyle waited at the podium, baton in hand, tapping it gently against the wooden stand. "Hurry up, everyone," she called. "We don't have much time." Parents and guests were already beginning to arrive. Maggie squeezed my hand before departing to the soprano section. She waved at Jack, who was already seated. He waved back and then waved at me. I smiled and sat down in my chair. My insides gnawed a little.

"Excuse me." Woolley crossed in front of Beth and sat in the chair next to me. "I had a terrible accident on the way over here, and now I have to sing with the altos," he said. Miss Boyle heard him and laughed in spite of herself. "Get in your seat or you'll be with the sopranos," she said.

"Annie," he said quickly. He looked and smelled perfect. If ever there was an Apollo, certainly he was it. He lifted my hand, kissed it, kissed my wrist, my arm up to the elbow. "Will you marry me?" He flashed his perfect teeth at me. Some of the girls surrounding us tittered. "Here he goes," Norma Peterkin said.

I laughed. "How many girls have you asked?"

"You're the first today."

"Can't we be friends?" I offered.

"That's what I wanted to be sure of." He had lowered his voice almost to a whisper. "We are friends, aren't we, Annie?" The blue eyes were serious.

"We are friends, Woolley. Thank you," I said.

He nodded, and stood up quickly. "I must go sit with the *men!*" he said in a deep voice, and climbed over several people to get to his chair.

We practiced three songs including an alma mater song that we were to sing after our march. I loved this choir, loved Miss Boyle's careful direction, her insistence on perfection. Between songs I looked for Maggie. She was already crying silently, wiping an occasional tear with her handkerchief. She grinned and shrugged her shoulder as if to say, "What's the use of fighting it?"

The room filled with people. We stopped practicing. I watched for my family, whom I finally spied about halfway back in the hall. My father was already taking pictures with a small camera and a flash. The camera blinked nervously and erratically, having taken on my father's personality. I wanted to guffaw but kept it inside, where it bubbled lightly. My graduation was going to be satisfactory if not completely perfect.

The program began. The principal spoke; Wanda Mussen, the class valedictorian, spoke; a guest speaker, a bald man with rimless glasses, spoke. I didn't hear any of it. We sang earnestly. We marched and received our diplomas. I listened for my favorite people. Margaret Alice Connors. John Charles Wakefield. Thomas Alvin Woolley. They sounded so dignified, so adult.

The choir closed: "Alma mater dear, we bid our loyalty true . . ." There was a benediction, and then it was over. The alto section fell into a fever of hugs and well wishes. I

179

broke loose and hugged Maggie. Over her shoulder I caught Jack's eye in the bass section. We exchanged a smile. The boys around him shook hands and slapped each other on the back. Maggie released me and wiped her eyes again. "I'll see you tomorrow," she said.

She turned and called Jack's name, telling him she wanted to see her parents first and then she'd meet him onstage after. I didn't hear his reply. I had a solid ache in my stomach.

I couldn't find my own family. I wandered down through the auditorium, stopping long enough to hand my cap and gown to one of the teachers, who was collecting them. The tassel was mine to keep. I looked in the wide front lobby, back into the auditorium. I stood on the steps outside. It was dark except for the spotlights illuminating the front of the building. Once more I searched the lobby and auditorium. They simply weren't there. It occurred to me that they might have assumed I was riding home with Maggie.

I couldn't help feeling abandoned.

I decided to walk home. It was a warm evening. There was something at once sorrowful and noble about walking home from one's own commencement, and that matched my feelings exactly. I walked down to 13th East, crossed the street, walked to 6th South, and turned right. I whistled and swung my tassel. On 6th South, below 13th East, I gazed at the downtown skyline, the Walker Bank beacon blinking in blue to tell me it was a fair and cloudless night, in case I hadn't noticed it.

A familiar Chevrolet slowed down along side of me and cut suddenly into a driveway in front of me, blocking out the sidewalk.

"Are you *walking* home? Jack's head leaned out the window. Maggie peered over his shoulder.

"My parents must have thought I had a ride. Actually it's a nice night for a walk." They both stared at me.

"We were just on our way to your house," Maggie said. "Weren't we, Jack?" She nudged his shoulder.

"What for?" I asked.

Jack turned off the ignition. "To ask you to go to the dance with us," he said.

It was my turn to stare. "You mean the three of us?"

"It's only a dance. We're not going to shower together," Jack said lightly.

"You have to," Maggie continued. "We're not going without you."

"True," Jack said.

"This is Maggie's idea, and she railroaded you. I know how she operates," I said.

"We agreed on it *together,*" Jack emphasized. "We both want you to go. *I* want you to go."

"I do too," Maggie said.

"Three people can't go to a dance," I said rather feebly.

"Of course they can," Jack argued. "We'll share. First you dance with Maggie, then I will. Then you will. Then I will. We'll both get Maggie for an equal amount of time."

I laughed.

"After the dance we'll go up to Emigration Canyon and kiss each other wildly." Jack's eyes gleamed.

"We will not!" Maggie cried.

I didn't know what to say. It seemed so absurd.

Jack opened the door and stepped out and gestured for me to get in. He had on a new tie with his suit. I wanted to dance with him again. I looked at Maggie who waited expectantly. "Come on," she said.

"I'll have to stop and tell my family," I said, stepping into the front seat.

"We have the whole night, Annie Sehlmeier." Jack started the truck. "The whole splendid night."

Kaatje Tefsen
Domstraat 18
Utrecht, The Netherlands

Dear Kaatje,

I'm so sorry I missed your call last night, but you'll never believe where I was. I went to the graduation dance after all with Jack and Maggie. Three of us at a dance! Can you believe it? We danced together on the fast dances. No one could tell the difference anyway. On the slow dances, Maggie seemed to disappear each time. The three of us had our picture taken, Jack in the middle and Maggie and I on either side of him laughing into the camera. We ordered three prints. At 10:30, Maggie announced that she had to go home because Mac was expecting her to call. "My dad's already here," she announced blandly. I was just sick. I felt like I'd ruined her night by being there. "Please don't go," I pleaded. But Jack was amused. "Mac wants a wake-up call, does he?" he asked. He kissed her cheek. "Tell him hello from me," he said, "and thanks."

Maggie laughed. "You owe me," she said to him. "You both owe me. See you tomorrow," and she left. I stood there with my mouth open. Jack pulled me out to the dance floor. "That leaves you and me, baby," he said gangster style. I'm so happy, Kaatje.

Mother wrote down your arrival time on the calendar. July is a great time to be here. We celebrate Independence day on the 4th and Pioneer Day on the 24th and there are parades and fireworks and rodeos and cookouts and root beer, which you'll hate. It tastes just like medicine. Mac will be back from England by then. Jack suggested we get a huge group together and take you to Lagoon (an amusement park) one day. Father is taking us all to Bryce Canyon at the end of the month. And of

182

course, we will talk talk talk. There's so much about the past year that I haven't written you in letters. So much I want to tell you. Come with bells on, Kaatje. *Dag* until July.

Kiss, kiss, kiss<br>
Annie

P.S. No, I can't imagine Edo as an expectant father. Tell them both congratulations.

# ABOUT THE AUTHOR

Louise Plummer was born in the Netherlands and emigrated to America with her parents when she was five years old. She grew up in Salt Lake City. She and her husband, Tom, have lived in Cambridge, Massachusetts, St. Paul, Minnesota, and recently returned to Utah, where they live on a mountain with their four boys, Jonathan, Edmund, Charles, and Samuel. Mrs. Plummer has a master's degree in English from the University of Minnesota and currently teaches writing at Brigham Young University. *The Romantic Obsessions and Humiliations of Annie Sehlmeier* received honorable mention in the Third Delacorte Press contest for an Outstanding First Young Adult Novel.